D1491194

Strangers
in the House

Strangers in the House

by

JOAN LINGARD

LODESTAR BOOKS

E. P. Dutton   New York

First published in the U.S.A. 1983 by E. P. Dutton, Inc.,
2 Park Avenue, New York, N.Y. 10016

First published in Great Britain 1981 by Hamish Hamilton
Children's Books, Garden House, 57–59 Long Acre, London WC2E 9JZ

Library of Congress Cataloging in Publication Data

Lingard, Joan.
    Strangers in the house.

    "Lodestar books."
    Summary: Fourteen-year-old Calum's difficult adjust-
ment to his mother's remarriage, their move to Edinburgh,
and his thirteen-year-old stepsister is further compli-
cated by the breakup of his father's second marriage.
        [1. Remarriage—Fiction.   2. Scotland—Fiction]
I. Title.
PZ7.L6626St   1983   [Fic]   83-1714
ISBN 0-525-66912-4

Printed in the U.S.A.   First Edition   10 9 8 7 6 5 4 3 2 1

For Hilde and Norman
and
Adrian, Jacqueline and Heather

Chapter One

They travelled down from the Black Isle on the Friday
between Christmas and New Year. It poured all the way
blurring the lofty mountain scenery of the Cairngorms
and later the flatter, greener countryside of Central
Scotland.

"Black Friday," muttered Calum, as he stared at the
rain-washed windows.

His mother, Willa, did not hear, or rather chose not to.
She turned over the pages of a magazine which she was
not reading and from time to time glanced up at the racks
overhead to check that all their numerous pieces of
luggage were still there. And the pieces *were* numerous
since they were in the process of removing themselves
from the North-eastern part of the country down to
Edinburgh. There were more in the guard's van too, as
well as their large sheep dog, Hamish.

Calum's young sister Betsy was sitting opposite him.
She scribbled and drew and sang to herself; she played
Happy Families with her doll and jiggled about and
dropped cards which had to be retrieved from between
their feet under the table.

She put down a card and frowned. She looked into

1

space, then gently pinched her mother's forearm.

"What is it, Betsy?"

"Does Tom play cards?"

"I don't know, love." There must be a lot Willa did not know about Tom, thought Calum. She went on, "Though I daresay he might."

Her voice was warm and bright, as if hoping to give hope. Betsy was not to be so easily swayed. She considered for a moment, mouth pursed, before she made her pronouncement.

"I don't want a new daddy."

"Shush!" said Willa, since the train was an open-carriaged one and full of bored travellers yawning over crumpled newspapers. A few had already begun to look a little more alert.

"You've got a father anyway," said Calum. "You don't need a new one."

He was addressing his mother, not Betsy. But Willa was rummaging in her bag, producing a tube of Polo mints and peeling back the paper. Calum shook his head. Betsy took two and dealt herself another card.

"Mrs Pond," she announced, swinging her legs and kicking Calum just below the knee again. To her doll she said, "Have you got Mr Pond?"

"Well, does she?" demanded Calum of his mother. "Need a new father?"

"Tom's a very nice man and he'll be very good to you." Willa spoke as if she were reciting words learned by heart.

"We don't need him to be good to us."

"Will he give me pocket money?" asked Betsy.

"Of course."

"Will there be Smarties in Edinburgh?"

"Lots and lots."

Calum groaned, so that he could be heard. His sister would sell her soul for a packet of sweets. Of course she *was* only six years old and could not be expected to understand the wider implications of what was happening to them.

2

Willa leaned across the table. "You liked Tom, didn't you?" Her large eyes were appealing to him. She had a way of opening her eyes very wide. Calum looked away.

"He was all right." He picked up the book which he was also not reading.

Tom had come up for a long week-end about a month ago, so that they could get to know him. Or at least be introduced, as he had said, laughing. He laughed a lot drawing their mother into his laughter and away from them. They seemed to share private jokes. They talked for hours and walked by the sea holding hands. Calum had felt himself grow hot in the head when he saw them hand in hand. It was stupid at their age, he had said to his mother afterwards, and she had told him not to be such an old fuddy-duddy. She was only thirty-eight and even if she was sixty-eight why shouldn't she walk hand in hand with a man that she liked? Loved. When she had used that word Calum had turned and gone out into the cool darkening evening and walked by the sea himself, listening to its gurgle and splash and wondering how he could bear to live without the sound of it in his ears. Their whitewashed cottage was in the old seaport of Cromarty, right on the shore, and looked out over the Cromarty Firth. Not even the sight of the cranes and the oil drilling platforms under construction in Nigg Bay had managed to spoil the sea for him.

His father worked at Nigg, as a welder, his own father. He was married now to a woman called Linette and they had two children, one aged two and the other six months, and they lived in a caravan further round the coast from Cromarty on the Easter Ross mainland. On week-ends that his father was not working he would come and fetch Calum. Occasionally Betsy would go too, but not often, for she was not fond of the two small children, or of Linette. Linette said she was spoiled and that she wouldn't let any child of hers ask all those cheeky questions and poke her nose into everything. Then his father would say they couldn't blame Betsy could they?

Linette treated him, Calum, differently. She seemed to like him, she talked to him on a level, and confided that she was bored when his father was at work and she was left alone in the muddy field with all the other bored wives. Especially when it was wet, or misty, and you couldn't even see across the field. Until his mother went down to the Edinburgh Festival and met Tom Cunningham at a concert in the Usher Hall, Calum had hoped that Linette would get so fed up one misty day that she would pick up the children and go, and then his father would come back to Cromarty and to them. It was a dream that he had, but even when he was having it he knew it was only that.

So now they were going to live with this man who had turned to their mother during the interval of a New York Philharmonic concert and struck up a conversation. It all seemed so odd. It didn't seem right that a chance meeting at a concert should change all their lives. Calum shifted in his seat.

"Calum kicked me," yelped Betsy.

"You've kicked me plenty of times!"

"Now, children!"

How dare she lump him with Betsy and call him child? He was fourteen years old and in two years' time could leave school and *her* and go where he wished. He would go back to Cromarty.

"Want a game, Calum?" Betsy forgot differences quicker than he did. It took him a while to let things simmer down.

"No thanks."

"Oh, come on, Calum," said Willa. "You can't play with two."

"Oh, all right." Anything for a quiet life.

Betsy shuffled the cards dropping half of them once more and then dealt them, saying, "One for you and one for me," in her high clear voice. All the people round were watching, from want of anything better to do, and Betsy was aware of their attention. She smiled and eyed the onlookers from under her long auburn lashes. She made Calum feel frozen up inside.

They had bought the cards in Inverness. It was Willa who had lifted them off the shelf.

"Honestly, Mother!" Calum had exploded.

"Honestly what, Calum?" His mother had looked at him innocently.

"*Happy* Families!"

"It's only a game. I'm not trying to brainwash you."

It was the way her mind was working though, he was sure of that. She wanted to turn them into a Mr and a Mrs with three children.

"I want Mrs Dose the doctor's wife," demanded Betsy and shrieked with delight when he produced Mrs Dose complete with dressing gown and curlers yapping into a telephone.

Betsy squinted at the fan of cards which she held close to her chest and considered her next move. Calum looked back at the window.

The rain had slackened momentarily. Hedges, walls, houses, trees flashed by and were gone. This countryside felt different from the green fertile peninsula of the Black Isle which lay close to the sea and the sky. A few factories were appearing, more habitations. Edinburgh was a beautiful city, and Willa was certain that they would enjoy living in it. Calum had been there several times on holiday and enjoyed himself though not for a moment had he considered that he would ever live in the place.

One got used to most things, given time, said his mother. Would he get used to Tom Cunningham? And to his daughter?

There was a thirteen year old girl: that made everything worse. If she had been Betsy's age he could have ignored her. Her name was Stella. Even to say the name in his head depressed him. They had not met her, he and Betsy. His mother had of course and said that she was a very nice girl, very bright and lively. She was bound to say that she was nice. And the fact that she was bright and lively did not cheer Calum. She would be noisy and say clever things and laugh a lot like her father.

She was supposed to have come north with him on his visit but at the last moment had developed a headache and sore throat and had to go and stay with her Aunt Susie.

"I think it was genuine," Tom had said to Willa.

"Even if it wasn't you couldn't force her to come could you?"

"Of course not. We have to give them all time to grow into it."

Grow into it indeed! They had a hope. And what were they doing but forcing them now? His mother had told him that he had no choice, she was his guardian and since he was under age he had to come with her. She had said her mind was quite made up and she had a right to some happiness of her own.

The rain was slashing against the window again. Darkness had closed in early even for mid-winter.

He gave Master Rake the gardener's son to Betsy.

Had his mother been unhappy all the time she'd lived with him and Betsy? He knew of course that she had been for the first few months after his father had gone off with Linette but gradually her face had lost that tight look and her smile had come back. They'd had lots of good times together since then, sitting round the fire on wild winter nights listening to the wind howl, walking along the shore on soft summer days when she would sigh and say she loved this place. If she loved it why should she leave it? If Tom Cunningham wanted to marry her why didn't he come to Cromarty? He was a freelance journalist, with a living to earn, Willa had retaliated; his contacts were in the city.

Betsy won the game. She laughed and swung her legs to and fro.

"My legs will be black and blue by the time we get to Edinburgh," said Calum, rubbing his knee.

Willa consulted her watch. "Shouldn't be long now."

"I think I'll go and see how Hamish is."

Calum got up. He had been to see Hamish at least half a dozen times during the journey.

He moved along the swaying train towards the guard's van. Tables were littered with paper cups, empty beer tins, screwed up food wrappings. The air in the carriages felt used up.

Hamish was asleep face down on his paws but he must have sensed Calum approaching for he jumped up at once and began to bark high and nervously.

"It's all right, boy. It's not been much fun for you has it being locked up in here?" Calum felt his nose through the grille. "Wonder what you'll think of Edinburgh? Never mind, we'll only have to stick it out for a year and nine months and then we'll go back to where we belong."

Hamish whined and pushed his nose into Calum's hand.

In the van were stacked a few pieces of small furniture, his bicycle, Betsy's tricycle, several enormous parcels, and Willa's loom and knitting machine. His mother earned money by weaving and knitting. They had lived off that and the maintenance his father provided.

The guard came through the corridor and stopped to look at Hamish. "He'll be glad to get out of there. We'll be coming into Edinburgh soon."

Calum followed the guard back along the train. People were stretching and yawning and reaching up to the racks to pull down their luggage.

His mother and Betsy were jostling around in the aisle trying to sort things into bags.

"Pick up *all* the cards now, Betsy, or you'll be sorry later. Look, there's Mrs Snip under the table."

Betsy dived under the table, cracked her head and surfaced yelling.

"You'll survive," said Willa, rumpling the top of Betsy's head.

"What a nasty bump," said a woman opposite and held out a bag of black and white striped balls.

Betsy's smile returned and her hand went into the bag.

"Get the big case down would you, Calum?" said Willa. "You're taller than I am these days."

She stood beside him ready to catch the end of it. As he reached up he turned his head and spoke in a low voice which would be heard by no one else in the general hubbub of noise.

"I don't know why you had to do this. We were all right as we were."

Chapter Two

"It would be much nicer if you *were* to come to the station with me."

"For whom?"

"Oh go on, Stella!" Aunt Susie looked round from the cooker. "You'll feel better if you do."

"I don't want them to come here, you both know that perfectly well already."

"You're damned right we do!" said Tom. "You've never stopped telling us."

"And you've never stopped asking me."

Tom and Aunt Susie exchanged looks.

Stella turned and marched from the kitchen along the hall to the sitting room, her black pony tail jumping behind her. She liked the feel of it slapping against the back of her neck. She could have walked for miles.

She closed the sitting room door firmly. Earlier that afternoon she had been to a ballet lesson and still wore her blocked shoes. She went up on to her points. She had been having lessons since she was three years old and her teacher said she showed great promise.

The door opened, and in came Tom. She flicked her head from left to right, joined her hands above her head.

"Get down from that stupid pose and come and sit beside me!"

"It's not stupid," she said fiercely. She could be fierce.

"Stella, I haven't time to play games. Their train's due in soon. *Come here!*"

She came and sat beside him, tucking her feet lotus-fashion beneath her.

"Look, love, I know you don't like the idea of strangers coming into the house—"

"Can you blame me?"

"No, of course not. And I know I'm asking a lot of you. But I'm asking you to try and see it from my side too." She held her lips tightly together and she stared ahead. He went on, "Have you never thought I might be lonely at times?"

"You've had me. I've cooked for you—" Her bottom lip was becoming less rigid and her voice less controlled.

"I know, Stella, but it's not just a matter of cooking."

"When Mummy died you said you'd never want to marry again!"

"That was four years ago."

"So you've forgotten her that quickly?"

Stella looked at the photograph of her mother which stood on the piano. She was the image of her mother, everybody said so, except Aunt Susie who thought she looked like her father. He was dark also. Her mother had been a dancer before she married, had given up her career to have her.

"No, I haven't forgotten her and I never will." He held out his hand. "Please, Stella, I'm asking you to help me."

"But, Dad, I liked it, with just the two of us."

"And so did I."

"Why then—?"

"Surely you're old enough to understand!" He was on the brink of losing his temper. He flared up easily, as she did.

"I *hate* the idea of a stepmother."

"Don't think of her like that then. Just think of her as a friend."

"I'm sure I shall hate her no matter how I think of her."

He got up and left the room.

Stella went to the window and looked out over the dark city. Their flat was high above the Meadows, an open stretch of green which separated the old town from the Victorian suburbs. From their windows they could see the castle and the lion-shaped hill called Arthur's Seat, and in daytime the Firth of Forth and the blue hills of Fife beyond. She loved their view. And now her father was talking of selling the flat to get a bigger one or a house. The flat *was* too small for five people, that she conceded, having as it did only two bedrooms and a boxroom, a large kitchen and sitting room, but she saw no reason why it should have to accommodate five people or why they should have to move in order to accommodate them. And she was to share her room in the meantime with a six year old girl!

"You'll like her," her father had said when he came back from his week-end in Cromarty. "She's really engaging."

She hated small engaging children; they bored her.

"And Calum seems a nice lad. Quiet, not as much to say for himself as Betsy."

She did not care what he had to say for she would not listen.

The door opened and in came Aunt Susie wiping her hands down her blue and white striped apron.

"I suppose *you*'ve come to get at me now?"

"Dead right I have! I want you to stop being a baby and give your father a chance. And don't bother losing your temper with me for it'll get you nowhere! Now away and get changed and go with him."

"Why should I?"

"*Go!*"

"Oh all right!"

Stella slammed out of the room into her bedroom which already was taking on an unfamiliar air with the other bed placed against the wall. She had pushed it as far away from her own as she could and put a screen round her area made of an old clothes drying stand draped with pieces of material.

She changed into jeans and a sweater and, pulling out the elastic band, shook her hair loose. Then she brushed it vigorously until her arm ached.

The door bell pealed. She ran to open it hoping for a diversion. A telegram perhaps to say they weren't coming? After all, the woman might have cold feet at the last minute.

On the door mat stood Uncle Nick, Aunt Susie's husband, smiling and clutching two bottles of wine to his chest.

"Hello, Beautiful! Lovely smell! Chicken casserole? I bet Susie's making us a fine feast." He was always in a good humour and never noticed other people's bad ones.

Her father was in the hall putting on his coat. "Are you coming or are you not, Stella?"

"I'm coming." She said it as if she were still reluctant, although she had known deep down all along that she would go.

"Should I come too?" offered Uncle Nick. "You might need the space in my car."

"Thanks, Nick, but I think we'll manage. I've got the roof rack on."

Their car—an ancient Volkswagen 'beetle' which miraculously managed to go on passing its yearly test—was parked in the street outside. One of the doors would not lock but no one had ever tried to steal it so Tom had given up saying, "I must get that damned thing repaired."

Rain was bouncing off the pavement. They dived inside the car.

Every traffic light on the way to the station went against them. Tom sat with his back hunched drumming his fingers on the rim of the steering wheel whilst he waited for the red to change to amber.

"Stupid thing seems to be stuck! We're going to be late."

Stella said nothing. There was nothing she could say except apologise—she supposed it was partly her fault they were late—but she had no intention of apologising. She watched the windscreen wipers flicking to and fro and began to feel hypnotised. The red light was reflected in the wet street making it look as if a pot of paint had been spilt. She felt sick, and excited.

The car lurched forward. Her father had let the gear in too quickly. At the next red light they stalled and when he tried to start the engine again it coughed and spluttered and died.

"Blast! I forgot to get petrol this afternoon."

"You should get the gauge fixed, Dad."

"All right, you don't have to tell me! Get out and help me push the damned thing in to the kerb. Who the hell ever invented machines? We'll just have to leave it and get petrol later."

They had broken down at the junction of George IV Bridge and the High Street. It was a busy time of day: approaching five o'clock. Laden buses lumbered past, cars honked and swerved round them, and a policeman with water dripping off his cape came to give them a hand.

"We'll need to run, Stella."

Her father seized her hand and through the slanting rain they ran down the Mound and to Waverley station below. By the time they reached cover Stella had a stitch like a dagger in her side and her hair hung like seaweed down her back.

They were standing beside the newspaper kiosk, the three red-haired MacLeods, and they looked lost and bewildered. Like refugees who did not know where to go next. A mountain of luggage was heaped beside them.

Tom bounded forward, Stella hung back.

"Willa! I'm terribly sorry, love. We ran out of petrol . . ."

Her face lit up when she saw him. They moved into one another's arms and it seemed to those who were watching that they would never separate again.

Willa was laughing when they did. "You're absolutely soaking!"

"Just a trifle damp."

"I was beginning to think you weren't coming."

"You should have known better than that!"

She would soon get to know that her father was late for everything, thought Stella; even when he was not kept back by other people. She stared into the distance above the boy's head as if she were reading the Departures board. He had his hands behind his back and he was frowning down at his feet but the small engaging girl was staring straight at her, Stella, and grinning.

"Stella, come and meet Willa."

They shook hands in turn, awkwardly. Stella hoped there was no one in the station whom she knew.

"You look like Hamish does when he's been swimming," said the small girl to Stella.

"Hamish is our dog," explained Willa.

As if on cue, Hamish barked.

"It's all right, Hamish," said the boy, bringing his right hand round to the front, revealing that it held a lead on the end of which was a large black and white sheep dog. It opened its mouth and barked loudly but whether in pleasure or alarm it was difficult to know.

Tom was staring at the dog as if he had seen a ghost. Willa was still smiling.

"I didn't know you were going to bring the dog with you, Willa?"

"We couldn't leave him behind, Tom."

Chapter Three

When Calum wakened next morning in the stuffy win-
dowless room—the dirty skylight twelve feet above his
head could scarcely be called a window—the only familiar
thing was the feel of Hamish lying across his feet. The
room scarcely deserved to be called that either; cupboard
would be more appropriate. He would get a proper room
of his own when they moved, so he had been told.

Opening his eyes and letting them adjust to the gloomy
light, he felt as if he was surfacing from a dream. Night-
mare would be a better word. And it wasn't over yet. The
events of yesterday evening seemed unreal. Getting themselves and their possessions transferred from Waverley
Station to this flat three floors up had been drawn-out and
exhausting. Tom had telephoned Uncle Nick who came
with his car, but they had had to make three trips to collect
everything and it was Calum who had had to wait in the
cold grey station to guard the stuff that remained. When
his turn came to go his feet felt like breeze blocks and
Hamish was whining with hunger.

The chicken casserole was dried up by the time they
came to eat it, sitting round the big wooden table in the
kitchen. Their first meal as a family, said Tom. Willa was

the only one who responded. "The first of many," she said, and they smiled at one another. Honestly! Calum had never heard her talk like that before. And the way they kept smiling at one another was enough to make you want to puke. They had all been too tired to talk or eat, except for Aunt Susie and Uncle Nick, and of course Betsy. It took a lot to dampen her down. She sat on Uncle Nick's knee and pulled his golden-red beard and laughed when he tickled her; she skipped with a rope up and down the long passage; she investigated every room, which did not take long, and looked inside all the drawers of the sideboard. She went on like a spinning top until all of a sudden she collapsed and had to be carried off to bed.

The Cunninghams had not slept in the flat: Aunt Susie and Uncle Nick took them away to spend the night in their cottage on the moors fifteen miles outside the city. The cottage sounded nice, and the moors too, except that you wouldn't be able to see the sea.

They were all to meet up again at the Registry Office at twelve noon.

Calum sat up disturbing Hamish who rolled over and resumed snoring. Surely his mother wouldn't go through with it? Did she really fancy that girl as a stepdaughter?

He swung his feet down and encountered cold linoleum. His slippers had not yet been unpacked. He went in pyjamas and bare feet into the passage which contained no less than nine doors, most of which must conceal cupboards. All were closed except for one which opened on to the sitting room. This was a fine room, large and light with its open view of city and sky, although at the moment there was little space to move around. They had used it as a dumping ground.

"What a lot of stuff!" Tom had said, rumpling the back of his hair with his hand as he surveyed it.

"There *are* three of us, Tom."

"I wasn't complaining, Willa!"

Calum's bicycle and Betsy's tricycle had been left

16

downstairs chained to the railings. Remembering that now, Calum tiptoed to the front door and opened it quietly. He peered over the bannister rail down into the grey well of the stair. The bottom looked a long way down. His mother had already given Betsy a lecture on taking care on the stairs and not leaning over and not for a second to think she could slide down the bannisters or she would kill herself. He could just make out the glint of handlebars below. There was nothing to be heard except for a faint scratching sound. A cat maybe, wanting to be let out. He would have to take Hamish out soon. They could no longer open the door and release him into the garden. They could no longer open a door and sniff the morning. The smell of the stair was a long way removed from that of sea and fresh air: it was musty and dank.

"Calum, is that you out there?" His mother was peering round the door. "Come in before you get your death of cold in those bare feet!"

She had lit the gas fire in the kitchen and put on the kettle. Whilst she made toast she hummed to herself.

"I know it's a big shake-up for you, Calum, but don't you think it's quite exciting as well?"

"Not particularly."

"Oh you! You can be such a stick-in-the-mud at times."

He crouched in front of the fire warming his hands. In fact, he did find it quite exciting, or would have done if they could have been here on their own—then it might have seemed a real adventure—but somehow or other he could not say that to his mother.

"I didn't know we would be living in a flat."

"Of course you did! I told you, I'm sure I did."

"No, you didn't. You called it a house. I remember you saying it was a light house."

"That's just a manner of speaking. People who live in flats refer to them as houses. At least in Scotland they do. You should know that!"

"How *should* I? I've never known anyone who lived in a

flat before. Not a tenement flat."

"Anyway, perhaps we *shall* move to a real house."

After breakfast Calum took Hamish for his walk. The rain had cleared to give way to colder, crisper weather. There were few people on the Meadows. They ran across the frost-spiked grass and Hamish barked and sniffed the air seeming to enjoy it as much as he had the air of the Black Isle. The fresh breeze whipped back Calum's hair and made his cheeks tingle. He felt better outside. He always did.

At the Registry Office he felt sucked back into the dream again. Listening to his mother repeating the declarations, *I, Willa MacLeod, do solemnly and sincerely declare that I know of no legal impediment to my marrying,* he felt that he could still not take in what was happening. Only a moment before his thoughts had drifted away and he'd been imagining himself out in the boat with old Angus the fisherman who liked to talk about the old days long before oil came to the North Sea. And then he was jerked back into this roomful of strangers by the sound of his mother's clear soft voice making promises to a man they hardly knew. Whom *she* hardly knew. Well, she couldn't really know him could she? They'd only seen one another a few times.

A ring was slipped over her finger and she was no longer Willa MacLeod but had exchanged her name for that of Cunningham.

Calum saw that Stella Cunningham sat with her mouth pursed and her shoulders hunched throughout the proceedings. She sat like a statue.

The ceremony over, the guests milled around the bride and groom. Calum and Stella hung back on the fringes of the crowd until called forward. He kissed his mother's cheek since it was expected of him and shook Tom's hand. Betsy was leaning against her new stepfather's side and beaming as if for a photograph.

They had lunch in an Italian restaurant with two

18

of Tom's newspaper friends, Aunt Susie and Uncle Nick and another relative, a great-aunt, who wore a hearing aid and spoke in a very loud voice. Calum was at the end of the table opposite Stella and Aunt Ethel.

"Your father could have taken his pick," said Aunt Ethel to Stella in what she meant to be a confidential whisper. "I mean, she's not bad looking but she's not what you'd call pretty exactly. Not with all those freckles."

Calum almost choked on his lasagne. He had just been thinking how pretty his mother looked and how young, with her laughing eyes and flushed face. Too good for Tom Cunningham by half!

"Fancy taking on two more children! Of course he always was irresponsible. Acts on impulse, regrets it later. He'll regret this, you mark my words, Stella. It's not as if he earns a fortune. Well, you know that yourself!"

"Aunt Ethel, *please!*" said Stella, whose face was scarlet to the edges of her cheek-bones. She caught Calum's eye and glanced away at once, disdainfully.

Calum pushed aside his plate and took a sip of the dark red wine in his glass. Maybe it would be an idea to get drunk! Tom seemed to be drinking a lot; he kept refilling his glass and those round about and calling for another bottle. If he were to turn out to be an alcoholic then his mother might leave him. And what was this about money? Calum hoped they were not going to have to worry about that as well. They had done enough of it in the past when his mother had sat at her knitting machine until her arms ached and her eyes were ready to drop out of her head. And if Tom didn't earn much money how was he going to buy a new house?

In the evening they had a party in the flat. More of Tom's friends came, carrying brown paper bags which clinked; some came with wives or girlfriends, some in groups of three or four. The neighbours from across the landing were asked in, and those who lived below.

"Tom loves parties," said Aunt Susie who spent most of the time in the kitchen making food, although she appeared not to mind. People came in and out and perched on the end of the table to talk to her. Everyone seemed to know everyone else—it was not long before Betsy could be counted in that category—apart from his mother and himself.

Calum sat at the kitchen fire with Hamish.

"Must be rather overwhelming for you, Calum," said Aunt Susie during a lull and they were on their own together.

He shrugged.

"Things'll quieten down though, I wouldn't worry, and then you'll all get a chance to know one another. Here, have a sausage roll! They're hot."

She took one and she gave a piece to Hamish who wolfed it eagerly. She stroked the dog's head.

"He'd enjoy the moors. You must bring him out to visit us soon."

She got up to welcome a man with a drooping moustache whose name was Bill. He appeared to have been drinking quite a lot: his voice was slurred.

"This one of the youngsters then?" Bill shook his head. "Tom's got a big heart, I must say that for him."

"I'm tired," said Calum. "I think I'll go to bed." He touched Hamish on the back of the neck and the dog rose.

"You won't get much sleep, lad," Bill called after him.

They were dancing in the sitting room. Before the party started they had piled some of the boxes up in one corner and put the rest in the bedrooms. His mother's knitting machine had found its way into his boxroom. He had to climb over it to get to the bed.

The music could be heard loud and clear. The whole flat was vibrating. Calum wondered how his mother was getting on and could not resist smiling to himself. She hated loud music, used to complain every time he turned the stereo up and tell him he would deafen himself before

20

he was twenty-one. Or else she would say the neighbours would be along to read the riot act. The neighbours here were at the party so there would be no one to ring the bell and object. And if the bell did ring it would probably not be heard.

He took out the science fiction novel he had brought with him on the train and to the accompaniment of the music and the sound of voices and peals of laughter began to read. Some time later, with his shoes on and the book resting on his chest, he fell asleep.

Chapter Four

When Stella returned to her bedroom after the wedding lunch she exploded. The child had more or less taken over the room: her possessions invaded every corner. She had moved the clothes dryer closer to her own bed, tossed aside Stella's pieces of material and arranged her dolls' clothes on the rails. The dressing table was covered with a doll's tea set; dolls, teddy bears and furry animals sat on ledges and shelves, their button eyes glinting. Stella could almost have sworn they were laughing. At her.

She went at once to find her father. He was in the kitchen surrounded by people. She stalked back to the bedroom and began to rearrange the room to her own liking. She bundled the dolls, plastic teapots, packets of cards, games in boxes, picture books, on top of the child's bed and the floor around it.

As she was dragging the clothes stand back to where it had stood before, the child appeared and began to make a scene, which was only what Stella had expected.

"How dare you touch my things!"

"You touched mine! And mine were here first. This is *my* bedroom."

Even as she was shouting the words Stella knew she ran

the risk of being told she was behaving like a six year old herself but could not help it. The child had to be told.

"My dolls need their clothes hung up."

"You can hang them over the chair beside your bed."

"I have to hang my own clothes there."

The argument was terminated, for the meantime, by the arrival of Stella's father and Betsy's mother.

"Stella, really, I'm surprised at you!" said her father.

"You must learn that you cannot have things all your own way, Betsy," said her mother.

"She threw my dolls on the floor. They're crying!"

"They were all over the place!"

"No they weren't."

"Yes they were."

"For goodness sake, Stella, do you think we have to have this on our wedding day?"

"You mustn't blame Stella, Tom," said Willa, which should have made Stella warm to her but didn't. Her father blamed her and that was what mattered, and it was Willa's fault that they were having a row at all. "Betsy will have to learn that other people have rights too," Willa finished up.

And there the dispute rested, to be taken up again later. Every time Stella went out of the room Betsy moved her stuff and whenever Stella returned she moved it back.

"You're lucky I don't throw it out of the window."

"Don't you like me?"

"Not very much."

"We'll sort it all out tomorrow, Stella," said her father. "When we've got peace and quiet."

"There will never be any peace and quiet in this house again!"

Stella sat on her bed for a while keeping guard. She wrote in her diary, putting down all she felt and thought. Most of it was violent.

The child did not come back: she had forgotten her dolls and their clothes and tea-sets and was enjoying herself at the party. When Stella felt calmer she went back and joined the party herself. The sound drew her. She liked people and her father's friends always made a point of talking to her. They treated her as an adult. Before the marriage several of them confided that they thought Tom was mad taking on another family and they felt it wasn't fair to her. But now she saw these same people were talking to Willa and laughing with her.

"Willa's nice," said Mungo, her father's special friend who worked for the BBC. "You'll be all right with her, Stella."

"I'm glad you think so!"

She felt betrayed by everybody except Great-Aunt Ethel who was an embarrassment to have as an ally. Tomorrow she would spend the day at her best friend Felicity's and tell her every little thing she had had to endure so far.

"You see, the trouble is that *she* is six and I am thirteen and so I come out of it as a big bully if I stand up for myself. I can't win."

Felicity thought the MacLeods sounded horrific, even worse than they had feared, and agreed with Stella that she could not be expected to put up with a spoilt brat like Betsy sharing her bedroom. Felicity was an even-tempered girl; she listened without interrupting and watched Stella's face with her steady gaze. She had restful grey eyes. She had a calming effect on Stella.

Stella sighed and lay back on Felicity's bed linking her hands behind her head. Felicity had a spacious, peaceful bedroom which she never shared with anyone except herself, Stella, when she came to stay for the night. The Halls lived in a big Victorian stone house with a walled garden surrounding it. Lilac and laburnums overhung the wall and a gean tree stood at the back of the garden. Felicity had an older brother and both her parents were musicians. No one ever seemed to quarrel in this house.

Stella commented on that now.

"Don't you believe it!" Felicity laughed. "We can fairly let rip when we get going."

Stella did not believe that. Mrs Hall believed in self control and the power of reason.

Felicity met the MacLeods when she came to tea. Calum said very little; Betsy talked too much. After they had done the dishes the girls went into Stella's bedroom so that they could discuss the MacLeods further but found Betsy already installed there feeding her collection of dolls and animals. Tom and Willa were in the sitting room, and Calum was in the kitchen.

"There's only the bathroom left," said Stella. "Or outside."

They chose the latter. With their duffel coats buttoned tightly across their chests and hoods up, they trudged up and down the paths on the Meadows, heads lowered against an icy wind. A few flakes of snow were beginning to drift down from a black sky.

"You see how crazy it all is," shouted Stella.

Felicity nodded vigorously.

"And did you notice how they're all covered with freckles?"

"Only on their noses."

"Can't hear you."

Felicity repeated what she had said but the wind whipped her words away again. The flakes were thickening; the paths were turning white. Felicity soon went home.

Stella complained to her father about Betsy taking up so much space. "And I can't even do my ballet exercises!" Tom sympathised. He knew that something would have to be done—and so did Willa—and they would do it once New Year was over and life returned to normal.

On Hogmanay they had another party and all the same people came who had been to the other one, as well as a few others, and Stella had some of her school friends in too, Felicity of course, and Pam Dickson and Jackie White. Long before midnight struck Calum disappeared into his boxroom and closed the door.

"Not very friendly is he?" said Pam.

"I think he looks O.K.," said Jackie.

Pam and Jackie had spent a long time admiring Hamish and stroking his fur. Sucking up to Calum, Stella considered, wondering why she had bothered to ask them. Not that they had got anywhere with their toadying for he had stared over their heads and answered in monosyllables.

"He must be the strong silent type," giggled Jackie.

Which was not how you could describe Jackie, thought Stella.

On New Year's morning Betsy wakened Stella early— much too early—by pulling back the corner of her Downie and asking what she wanted for breakfast.

"What?"

"Orange or apple juice?"

"Orange," muttered Stella.

Betsy brought the juice in a pink plastic cup and six Smarties on a pink plastic plate.

"Now sit up and eat your breakfast, there's a good girl."

Half-dazed with sleep, Stella sat up and drank from the pink cup. Through the wall Hamish whimpered and then Calum was heard talking to him. The boxroom door opened. The boy and his dog were going for their morning walk.

Betsy tugged the curtain aside and watched them from the window. She laughed.

"Calum is putting footprints all over the snow. And so is Hamish. Look, Stella, come and see!"

Stella slid further down into her warm bed. She felt as if these strangers were putting footprints all over her head.

"I'm going out to build a snowman," cried Betsy. "The biggest snowman you ever saw."

"You'd better go and ask your mother first."

Tom did not relish being wakened so early on New Year's morning. He had not gone to bed until five. His groans travelled along the hall. Serves him right, thought Stella.

Betsy was allowed to go downstairs as long as she promised to stay beside Calum and Hamish. In red wellington boots she went hopping down the three flights shouting that she was going to build the biggest snowman in the world.

Now that Stella was thoroughly awake she felt she might as well get up. On her way along the corridor to the bathroom she heard Tom and Willa talking. Their bedroom door was ajar.

Stella stopped to fix her slipper.

"I hope we haven't been too selfish, Tom."

"Don't be silly, love. Haven't we got a right to make a life for ourselves too?"

"Of course. But the children—"

"One day they'll grow up and leave us."

"Yes, but in the meantime—"

"They'll survive. Kids are adaptable. In no time at all we'll be just like any other family."

Stella tiptoed the rest of the way into the bathroom and locked the door behind her. Any other family indeed! How could her father imagine that they would ever turn into a family like the Halls? Or the Whites or Dicksons for that matter? Jackie's and Pam's families were forever having their ups and downs, they had shouting matches and Pam's father kept losing jobs and upsetting his wife's ulcer, but you could see that they all belonged together. There was no chance that the five of them—Cunninghams and MacLeods—would ever do that.

That day Willa tried to engage Stella in conversation. Stella knew that she was trying to and felt herself closing up like a clam. She wished she did have a real live shell, a hard one, to cover herself with. Instead she folded herself up into the lotus position, clasped her hands on her lap and stared straight ahead.

"I'd like us to get to know one another and be friends, Stella."

Why did they have to keep saying things like that? Stella had heard her father doing it to Calum as well and he'd got nowhere either. Of course getting anything out of Calum was like trying to squeeze blood out of a stone. The only person he talked to was his dog.

Willa sighed. "I know it's a very difficult situation for everybody and I feel so clumsy."

Stella glanced away from the large and appealing amber-coloured eyes. No doubt it had been by looking like that at her father that she had managed to trap him into asking her to marry him.

"Trap him?" said Aunt Susie and laughed, when Stella voiced her thought. She had gone to stay with her aunt and uncle for a couple of days before going back to school. "I don't think anyone would trap your father against his will."

Uncle Nick put another log on the fire. Flames licked round it making it hiss and crackle. The burning logs were making a delicious smell in the low cottage room. Outside, a thick blanket of snow enveloped the countryside. Stella sighed and subsided into the deep, red velour chair. She did not want to talk about the MacLeods any more. She had come to get away from them, and as the sun lowered in the winter sky sending streaks of pink and green across the snowy fields she found that she could scarcely remember what they looked like. Except that they had dark red hair and freckles.

"I love being here."

She felt so drowsy and peaceful that she thought she would never manage to get out of the chair again.

"You can come any time you want," said Aunt Susie. "You know that."

"Aunt Susie—" Stella hesitated. She sat up a little straighter. An idea had just come into her head, a marvellous idea, and she could not understand why she had not thought of it before. It would solve all their problems.

"Aunt Susie, do you think I could come and live here with you and Uncle Nick?" She held her breath.

Aunt Susie and Uncle Nick exchanged glances in the infuriating way that older people did.

"But Stella love, you'd miss your friends—"

"No, I wouldn't. Felicity could come and stay at weekends and I could stay at her house sometimes."

"There's school too though. And your ballet. You wouldn't want to give that up, would you?"

"Of course not! I wouldn't have to. I could come into town with you and Uncle Nick every day. Well, couldn't I? You go in and out to work. Oh please say yes! Please! I hate it so much at home. I can't bear it!"

"Your father would miss you," said Uncle Nick quietly.

"No, he wouldn't. He doesn't care about me any more. He only cares about *her*. And I hate her!"

"I doubt if you really do," said Aunt Susie. "And your father would be very unhappy if you left him."

Stella did not believe that. "If he cared about me he wouldn't have married her. Ask him if he'll let me come here and see what he says! He'd be pleased, I know he would."

"I have no intention of asking him," said Aunt Susie. "Stella, we love you dearly, but it is quite out of the question for you to come and live here with us."

"But why?"

"Apart from the fact that your place is with your father, you must realise that we have our own lives to lead, Nick and I."

Chapter Five

Apart from having to leave Hamish all day, Calum did not mind the opening of the school term. It was not that he particularly relished the idea of being a new boy at his age, but he was glad to have something to do outside the house which was constantly filled with noise, people and objects, and he welcomed the idea of having some kind of pattern to his days again. He liked the days to have a rhythm, like the sea.

Stella hated school, or so she said, though when he saw her in the corridors in the middle of a bunch of girls she was always talking and laughing. She liked to be dramatic, to make extreme statements. If she was cold she declared she was frozen; if she was hungry she was starved. She said that school bored her—not to him directly, usually to her father who did not pay too much attention—and that most of the teachers were mentally defective. It was one of her favourite phrases at the moment: mentally defective.

Calum was bored in some classes; in others interested. When he was bored he let his mind drift away; he travelled northwards and crouched again beside the white-flecked curling waves and listened to the screech of the gulls. He watched them swooping in low over the water and the swans feeding along the edge of the shoreline. He inhaled the smell of seaweed and of dark brown earth.

"Have you ever thought of doing marine biology when you're older?" asked the biology teacher. Biology was one of the classes in which Calum did not dream.

"No."

"You should. Since you're good at biology and keen on the sea. It would bring your interests together."

Calum found a book in the library which he read during breaks and between classes whilst his fellow pupils kicked up a din. He shut out the noise. He was getting good at excluding sounds he did not wish to hear.

After the first couple of weeks the pupils in his classes accepted him. He was polite to those who were polite to him and ignored those who were not. He could stand up for himself physically if he had to: he was no weakling, being tall and broad-shouldered. One day a boy tried to trip him up in the corridor, and failed. Calum walked on without looking back. He was slow to rise but when he did he took a long time to cool off.

In the science classes he worked beside a thin dark boy called Daniel who was going to be a physicist when he grew up. They talked only of the work they were doing and when they passed in the corridor they merely nodded.

At lunch time Calum went home to give Hamish a short run. The dog hated being shut up in the flat and was full of pent-up energy when Calum arrived.

"He hears you coming from the bottom of the stairs," said Willa.

"It's all right, boy, it's all right!" Laughing, Calum quietened Hamish who danced on his hind legs barking and trying to lick Calum's face.

After school they had a really long run in the Queen's Park where Hamish could be let off the leash and run free, as long as they stayed away from the area where the sheep grazed. Sometimes they climbed to the top of Arthur's

Seat, which sat in the middle of the park; from there they looked down at the city and beyond to the Firth of Forth and the Fife coast.

"Up there's Cromarty, Hamish. We'll be going at Easter. For two whole weeks! Or perhaps longer. Who knows—it might be longer."

Hamish barked with enthusiasm.

"The city's not for us, is it, boy?"

Calum wrote to tell his father that things were not working out. 'I have to live in a room not much bigger than a cupboard without windows. The flat is three flights up and there's no garden except for a big piece of ground called a back green where the women hang their washing. If I take Hamish into it the old woman who lives on the ground floor bangs on her window and yells at me. Mother seems all right and Betsy is her usual self.'

Betsy had settled into her school after ten minutes. The first afternoon there she brought home five other small girls who played "Chasey" up and down the hall and in and out of the bedroom and kitchen, shrieking.

"I can't stand this racket," said Tom after half an hour and went out.

"She's got to have somewhere to bring her friends," said Willa, biting her lip, after he had gone.

"Of course she does," said Calum, although if it had not been for Tom he would have said that he thought that the noise was a bit much too. But he would never take Tom's side, not even to the smallest degree, against his mother.

Tom did most of his work at home, usually sitting at the table in the kitchen where it was warmer than his bedroom, so when Betsy came home just after three he had to pack up or else lug his typewriter up the hall to the sitting room and see if he could find a space there. He would drop papers and swear, and the typewriter's carriage would shift up and down since he'd forgotten to lock it. Half the time he said it wasn't worth the trouble.

Willa's loom and knitting machine had stayed in the

sitting room. Where else could they go? She was knitting
striped jerseys for a shop in Stockbridge, on the other side
of town. The colours were lovely: every shade of the
rainbow. She was making one for Stella in different tones
of pink, purple and orange.

"Don't work your fingers to the bone now," said Tom.

"I won't. But we do need the money, don't we? After all,
there are five of us."

"There are indeed."

He smiled at her. Whenever they smiled at one another
Calum felt he was intruding and would get up and leave
the room. His mother did not talk to him as much as she
used to. How could she, with Tom beside her most of the
time? Calum was glad that Tom did often go out between
four and six. The dead time of the day, Tom called it. He
went to the pub when it opened at five. Calum liked that
time of day; he came home, had a cup of coffee with his
mother and they talked, and then he had his long outing
with Hamish. In their other life his mother had turned to
him every time she had something on her mind; now she
turned to Tom.

'I'm sure Mother wouldn't mind if I didn't live with her
all the year round now,' he wrote in another letter to his
father who had not yet replied to the first. He was a
terrible correspondent. 'In the evenings she goes out a lot
with Tom or else Tom's friends come in. I don't see a great
deal of her.'

The last sentence was a bit of an exaggeration, he
conceded as he contemplated it. But he did not change it.
He took the letter to the post before he would change his
mind.

When he came back he found that his bicycle had gone
from the bottom lobby. He could hardly believe it. He had
only been away for ten minutes.

"They're fly, these bicycle thieves," said the policeman
who came to take down particulars. He did not offer much
hope of recovery. "They have factories where they

33

dismantle the machines and put the pieces together again so that you wouldn't recognise them in a month of Sundays."

"But it had a chain on it."

"Ach, they'll have cut through that easily enough. Probably watching for you coming out. Whip the bike into the back of a van and they're off."

Betsy and her friends played at bicycle thieves until a new idea took their fancy.

Calum's bicycle was not found and, naturally, was not insured.

"We must start making provision for things like that," said Willa.

She took out Tom's insurance policies and found that the flat was insured for about a third of its value and the contents for next to nothing.

"What if we had a fire?" she said, horrified.

"O.K., O.K.," said Tom. "I'll increase the insurance."

"Bet he won't," said Stella after he had gone out. "He doesn't care about insurance policies and pensions and a steady income." And neither, from the tone of her voice, did she.

"That's all right as long as you're not up against the wall," said Willa.

At the end of January Calum received a letter from his father, a single page saying that he and Linette were fine, as were the children. He had been doing a lot of overtime at week-ends and the weather was lousy. The kids were stuck in the van most of the day. He did not answer any of the points in Calum's letter. It was quite probable that he had forgotten what Calum had said for he lived very much from moment to moment.

As Tom did too, Calum realised.

"You must go and see the Building Society, Tom," Willa kept saying and he would promise that he would, the next day.

"Tomorrow never comes," said Stella.

"Less of your cheek, madam!" said her father good-naturedly.

The sitting room, as well as housing extra furniture and the loom and knitting machine, remained cluttered with boxes whose contents could not find a home. Hanks of wool lay over the chairs, piles of paper were stacked on top of the piano.

"We shall *have* to do something about a new place or else have a really good clear out," said Willa, who had just spent an hour trying to reduce the clutter. She had had little success which had made her slightly irritable.

"O.K., O.K.!" Tom held up his hands. "I'll go and see the bank manager *and* the Building Society tomorrow. I promise!"

"There is no tomorrow," said Betsy.

"You're right, Betsy! But when tomorrow becomes today I shall go."

Calum came back early from his walk the following afternoon. His mother was in the kitchen drawing circles in red Biro round suitable properties in the *Scotsman* and the *Edinburgh Evening News*.

"A ground and basement flat could be all right, don't you think, Calum? Then we'd have our own front and back doors and a garden."

"Can't basements be damp?"

"Mm. Sometimes, I suppose. Depends on the basement. Here's a terraced house, sounds pretty good. Four bedrooms—we'd need that—sitting room and dining room. Tom and I could use the dining room as a workroom/study."

Stella came in. "Have you been looking at houses?" she asked in the off-hand way she adopted when she wanted to suggest she was not really interested.

"Not yet. Only at the ads so far. But I have rung up and made some appointments to view."

Stella sat down by the fire to take off her boots. "Did he

go?"

"Yes."

"Are you sure?"

"Are you trying to suggest I can't trust your father's word, Stella?" Willa tried to speak lightly.

"No. But he's got a bad memory. He meets people and starts talking."

"Well, as a matter of fact I was here when he rang up the bank and the Building Society to make the appointments."

"That's all right then." Stella glanced at the kitchen clock; it said half past five.

"I don't suppose he'll be back before six." Willa began to clear the table. She asked Calum to set it. Often she asked him to do things which she might have asked Stella to help with. And Stella never offered.

At six o'clock the dinner was ready. Here, they ate any time between six and seven, depending on when Tom came in. In Cromarty, they had eaten regularly at half-past five since they were always hungry and Betsy went to bed not long after seven. Or was supposed to.

"My tummy can't wait much longer," said Betsy at six-thirty. "It's got a big hole in it."

"Dad'll be in the pub, no doubt," said Stella.

"Yes, he usually likes to have a quick drink with Mungo before he comes home," said Willa.

"A *quick* drink?"

"I think we'll go ahead and eat."

Willa ate very little. She had her head cocked towards the door. Stella watched her from across the table.

She doesn't like my mother, thought Calum, with rising fury that threatened to choke him; she likes to see her suffer. He gulped down a drink of water.

"More meat, Calum?"

"No thanks."

"What's up with you? You've usually got such a good appetite."

Willa pushed it no further. She was not interested in his appetite at that moment anyway.

They cleared away the dishes and Betsy got out her painting book even though Willa protested that it was nearly bedtime and not worth her starting to make a mess. Calum laid his books at the other end of the table and began on his homework.

"Have you not got any homework, Stella?" asked Willa.

"I do mine in class."

"Can't be very good then can it?" Willa was still humouring her.

"Nobody's ever complained."

The bell rang and Stella went to the door saying she was expecting Felicity. The girls retired into Stella's bedroom and closed the door.

"You simply *must* go to bed soon, Betsy," said Willa.

"Can't. Not yet. I'm painting a big house. The one Tom's gone to buy for us."

"He hasn't actually gone to buy one yet. He's gone to ask if we can borrow the money to buy one."

Betsy licked the end of the paint brush and dipped it into the purple pot. "I think I'll make the door purple. With a yellow knocker. What colour curtains can I have for my room, Mummy?"

"I don't know, Betsy. We'll have to wait and see."

"Wait and see what?"

"What material there is in the shop." Exasperated, Willa got up, putting aside the jersey she was sewing together, and lifted the jam jar of water from the table. "That's quite enough now, Betsy! It's eight o'clock and you'll never get up for school in the morning."

"I've got to finish this bit, I've got to!"

Calum steadied his end of the table. He would have to rub out the last equation. It looked as if it had been done with an earthquake going on.

"I can't go to bed. Felicity's in my room."

"You have your own bit now."

A line had been drawn down the middle of the room and a four leaf folding screen bought for Stella which she used to protect her privacy as she called it. Betsy said it wasn't fair that she couldn't see Stella in her bed when Stella could look round the corner of the screen and see her.

Some twenty minutes later after more prevaricating Betsy went to bed.

"She's exhausting, that child!"

"You should be firmer with her, Mother."

"Don't *you* start, Calum!"

Stella and Felicity, in retreat from Betsy, arrived in the kitchen.

"Dad not home yet?" Stella knew very well that he was not.

"Not yet."

"Why don't you go into the sitting room?"

"It's cold in there."

"You can put the fire on."

"It takes ages to heat up."

"What are you doing, Calum?" asked Felicity, inclining her head.

"Biology."

"He's always swotting," said Stella.

Felicity's cheeks turned pink, but for what reason Calum could not guess. He couldn't guess much where these girls were concerned. Back home he had talked to one or two, about school, this and that. They had been different. And he had known them since childhood.

Perhaps Felicity felt she shouldn't have asked him anything. She said Hello in school if she was on her own, but not when she was with Stella.

Betsy came back three times, for a drink of water, to get her hot water bottle made hotter, and to say that she had forgotten to give her mother a note from the teacher.

Felicity left at nine o'clock and soon afterwards they heard Tom's key in the lock.

He came carrying a bunch of half-dead irises which he had bought in a Pakistani shop that stayed open late. "I'm sorry, Willa love, honestly I am! I met Mungo and there was this other chap with him who was able to give me a lead on that nuclear dumping story I'm working on."

Calum could not bear to look at his mother's face. He could smell the drink on Tom's breath.

"Did you see the bank manager?" she asked quietly. "And go to the Building Society?"

Tom slumped down into the chair beside the fire. "Yes, I did." He sighed. "Make me a cup of coffee, there's a love, would you, Stella?"

Stella, looking like a cat that has just finished licking a giant mixing bowl full of whipped cream, got up at once to fill the kettle.

"They said no?" Willa looked straight at Tom.

"I'm afraid so. They said I couldn't possibly get a bank loan or a bigger mortgage, not on my unpredictable earnings. They're not keen on people who work freelance, unless you're making pots of money."

"I see," said Willa, sitting down beside the table, still holding the half-dead flowers between her slim supple fingers.

Calum saw too, quite clearly: it meant that they would have to stay where they were, he in his boxroom without windows, and Stella sharing her bedroom with Betsy. In spite of that off-putting prospect, Stella did not seem perturbed. A little smile was hovering about her mouth as she poured her father's coffee and demurely put the cup into his hand. Perhaps she thought that after tonight Willa would give up, repack the boxes that had been unpacked, pick up her loom, knitting machine and children, and go.

Chapter Six

Willa did not go. She said that there was only one thing for it: they—she and Tom—would have to work as hard as they could and try to save some money to put towards the new house. She had had an order in that morning for twelve sweaters and a woven hanging.

"We can also economise a bit. We do tend to be extravagant, you know."

Economy had never featured much as a concept in Tom's life before. He had spent what he earned and when that ran out he did without for a while or else borrowed from Mungo or Bill. He and Stella had been known to live on potatoes and beans for a few days until the next cheque came in. Stella had griped a bit at the time but in retrospect it seemed a small price to have paid to have her father to herself. And there had always been great excitement when long-awaited money did come in. "Get your coat on, Stella. We're in the money again. Let's go out for a steak!"

There would be no going out for steaks with Willa in charge. She said she was used to managing on a small budget, so it wouldn't be a new experience for her.

She and Tom withdrew to their bedroom and talked for ages.

"I'm really sorry, Willa," Stella heard her father say as she went along the hall. They had a habit of not closing their door properly which had its advantages. "I know I should have come home earlier. But it won't happen again, I promise."

She burned inside hearing her father talk in such a meek and mild way to that woman.

"It was quite sick-making," she told Felicity next day. "She'll walk over the top of him if he's not careful."

"I can't imagine your father letting anyone do that."

"Only goes to show doesn't it?"

They were quiet for a moment, munching cheese and onion crisps. Stella sighed, squashed the crisp bag flat.

"I can understand her being annoyed though," said Felicity. "Well, I mean, she had cooked his dinner."

Felicity's father came home at the same time every night, and if by chance he was delayed he rang home in good time. There had been a time when Stella had thought that was marvellous; she no longer did. It was bad enough having a timetable at school without one at home as well.

"He doesn't mean anything by it though, Felicity. He gets carried away by what he's doing and forgets the time."

Felicity had turned her head. Calum was coming up the road towards the school, returning from lunch. He said, "Hello," as he passed, without exactly looking at them.

"He's mentally defective, if you ask me."

"He's just quiet, that's all. And he can't be very happy either."

"No, I suppose he can't," said Stella. She had not thought about that before. "Maybe he wants to go back to Cromarty as much as I want them to go back." If that was so it was a pity they couldn't get together and work on it. But getting together was quite out of the question. They were barely civil to one another and she knew he hated her as much as she did him.

41

When Stella confided in Aunt Susie she did not get much sympathy there either. Her aunt frowned and said she had hoped that Tom would have given up spending so much time in the pub now that he was married again.

"He doesn't spend *all* that much time," cried Stella, outraged. Everyone seemed to be against him. And her. The two went together. "You'd think he was an alcoholic." They had been having talks on teenage alcoholism in their Social Education class. It was becoming a serious problem, the teacher had informed them, his eye solemnly travelling along the rows as if he was seeking out potential addicts.

"No, he's not that. And I hope he never will be. But he has to watch himself, Stella. I think you're old enough for me to be able to say that to you."

Her aunt smiled at her though Stella could not see that there was anything to smile about. She felt let down by her father's sister. She ought to be on his side. Stella said so.

"But I am! That's why I want this new marriage of his to work out. When your mother died he began to drink quite heavily, you know. But you probably didn't. One couldn't blame him. And then journalists tend to drink more than the average. It's partly all the waiting about they have to do. And they live off their nerves."

Stella felt as if she was living "off her nerves", as Aunt Susie called it. In the sitting room the knitting machine clanked, in the bedroom Betsy made noises that ranged from humming to screaming, and in the kitchen Calum was silent. Even his silence irritated her.

"They make me want to scratch myself," she told Felicity. "I can't sit still when they're around." Which meant that she was seldom able to do so. She spent more and more time in Felicity's house. That, and the rather dusty church hall where the ballet school held its classes. As soon as she entered the room and heard the chattering of the gathered, waiting girls and the sound of the pianist warming up, she forgot the MacLeods.

"You mustn't abandon us altogether," said her father on a rare occasion when they were alone.

"*They* are driving me out of the house."

"Willa's bending over backwards to be kind to you." He was angry. "She's just finished knitting you a fantastic sweater—"

"She can't buy me with a sweater." She had put it away in the bottom of a drawer even though she did like the colours.

"She doesn't want to buy you, for heaven's sake! She's only doing her best to make a home. Why can't you do your best?"

She shrugged.

His anger collapsed; he looked sad. "Are you terribly unhappy, love?"

How could she say yes to that, especially when he was looking so miserable? She shrugged again, unable to say anything, letting him make up his own mind as to the extent of her misery. If only they could go back to how they had been two months before!

"Let's go out and have a cup of coffee together, shall we? And a big piece of Black Forest gateau?"

Her mood changed at once, as did his. They set off across the Meadows talking twenty to the dozen. He asked her about her ballet and she chattered on telling him all the little things that she had not had the chance to tell since the MacLeods came. The paths were busy with students walking home from university. Above the roof-tops and castle ramparts the sky was turning pink. She could not understand how anyone could hate living in Edinburgh. But she knew Calum did.

They went to a café in the Grassmarket and had two cups of fragrant coffee and a slice of gateau apiece. Outside the light was leaving the street; a misty greyness was creeping in between the buildings. They sat in the window and watched people passing. Willa had gone to collect Betsy from a birthday party and would be on her way home. They would come home and find that she and her father were out. To know that increased Stella's pleasure.

"Another piece of cake, Stella?"

"Yes please!"

She went to the counter to get it. She smiled at the girl serving and the girl smiled back.

Her father watched her eat. "We must do this more often."

She nodded.

When the last crumb was gone he looked at his watch and said he supposed they'd better go. Outside they ran into Mungo who said, "Time for a quick drink? No you can't, can you, not with young Stella here?" They stood for quite a while as Mungo had a story to tell Tom. A long story. Her father put his arm round her to protect her back from the wind; he hugged her close to him.

"Cold?"

She shook her head. She felt warm right to the centre of her body.

They said goodbye to Mungo and strolled back across the Meadows. Tom crooked his arm so that she could tuck her hand into it. It was dark now; the lights along the paths glimmered. She could have walked all night.

"There you both are!" said Willa when they came in. It sounded like a reproof but Stella was not in the least put down by it and neither was her father, she was happy to see. He laughed and said they'd been out boozing on coffee.

"What's boozing?" asked Betsy.

"Never you mind!" said Tom.

Willa began to dish out shepherd's pie.

"Not for me, thanks," said Stella. "I've just eaten two ginormous pieces of Black Forest gateau."

Willa opened her mouth to say something, then decided not to.

"I want Black Forest," said Betsy, pushing away her plate. "Don't like that. It's horrible."

44

Willa pushed the plate back. "Eat your dinner up and don't be silly!"

Betsy pushed the plate back again, slopping some mince over the edge on to the cloth.

Willa smacked her hard across the back of the hand. Stella winced, as if she herself had been slapped, and knew that it was she whom Willa would have liked to slap. Betsy burst into tears and rushed from the room screaming.

Willa sat down. "She's got to learn." She put a hand to her head.

She and Tom and Calum ate their shepherd's pie in silence. As soon as she could Stella asked to be excused and left the table. She put on her coat and walked up to Felicity's house. Willa made her feel black inside. But the marriage could not last much longer, she reckoned. Great-Aunt Ethel said she'd give it six months at the outside.

In the middle of February Tom and Willa decided to go skiing at Aviemore for a few days.

"You don't mind, do you?" asked Willa.

"No," said Calum, though the word almost seemed to choke him.

"We can do with a break from you lot," said Tom with a grin. "And we didn't have a honeymoon."

"Can I stay at Felicity's?" asked Stella.

"I want you to stay here, Stella," said Tom. "Aunt Ethel's coming to look after you all."

Stella argued but her father would not give way.

"Why can't Aunt Susie and Uncle Nick come?"

"They're busy."

Willa shouted reams of instructions into Aunt Ethel's ear before she left, particularly about Betsy. To Calum she said, "You will keep an eye on her, won't you?" And Tom told Stella he was relying on her. To do what? she wondered. Keep the peace? That didn't depend on her alone. With Betsy her conflict erupted regularly; with

45

Calum it took the form of cold war.

In fact, it was more peaceful with Tom and Willa out of the way. Aunt Ethel did not care if they were all being nice to one another, nor did she notice. She sat by the kitchen fire embroidering a tray cloth, oblivious of the arguments that raged over territorial rights in Stella and Betsy's bedroom. Betsy would never give up. Every day she tried to gain another inch, or more usually a yard. She brought home large sections of her class to partake of juice and Smarties from the pink plastic tea-set. Calum frequently had to walk the little girls home afterwards as Betsy had promised that he would, or else their mothers would not have let them come.

"It's amazing how she gets her own way," said Stella as she and Felicity walked home together, stopping off at the butcher and greengrocer since Stella was doing the shopping again. The shopkeepers said they had wondered where she'd got to. They had missed her.

Felicity came up for a cup of coffee. The flat was amazingly quiet: Aunt Ethel was embroidering, Calum had gone for his afternoon walk with Hamish, and Betsy was playing in someone else's house for a change.

The girls took their coffee into the sitting room where the gas fire glowed warmly. Aunt Ethel must have been in earlier and forgotten to turn it off. She was very forgetful, which had its uses.

Felicity looked at the half-completed hanging on Willa's loom. "It's lovely isn't it?"

Stella didn't look. She made a point of not looking at anything Willa did.

They forgot Willa and chewed over school gossip which they could do for hours on end. They had fallen out with Jackie White who had passed on a piece of confidential information given to her by Stella. "She's a real little sneak!" They couldn't understand how they had ever liked her.

Time slipped comfortably by: they grew drowsy in front

46

of the fire. Felicity yawned and said she should be going but she did not go. The front door opened and they heard Calum and Hamish come in.

"It's O.K., boy, I know you're thirsty."

A minute later Calum put his head round the door and said, "Your aunt's burning something in the kitchen."

They ran to the kitchen to find that Aunt Ethel had boiled the carrots dry. An acrid smell hung in the air. Stella scraped the burnt vegetables into the bucket, in spite of Aunt Ethel maintaining there was nothing wrong with them, and scoured the pan with a Brillo pad.

"I really must go," said Felicity. "It's nearly six o'clock."

"*Six?*" said Calum. "Where's Betsy?"

"Playing at somebody's house," said Stella.

"Whose?"

Stella asked Aunt Ethel, twice, "What was the girl called, Aunt Ethel?"

"Let me think now. Hazel. Yes, I'm sure it was Hazel."

Stella could not recall any of the small girls who played in her bedroom being called Hazel but then she paid as little attention as possible to them. Six o'clock came and went, Felicity departed saying she hoped Betsy would come in soon, and she would keep an eye open for her on her way home.

Aunt Ethel brought a scorched steak pie from the oven and set it on the table.

"I think maybe I should go and look for Betsy," said Calum uneasily. "She didn't say where Hazel lived did she?"

"No, she did not. I presumed *you* would know," said Aunt Ethel, as if it was his fault for not knowing. "Sit down and have your dinner first. I'm famous for my steak pies am I not, Stella?"

"Are you?" said Stella, but her great-aunt did not hear. She was thrusting the knife into the thick black-edged pastry and saying that she knew that they must have

47

enormous appetites at their age. It was fortunate that Hamish was lying under the table. He was as good as any vacuum cleaner.

"Did she say what time she'd be back?" asked Calum.

"Who? Your sister? She may have done. She talks too fast for me. But I think she said she was having her tea there."

"Why didn't you say so before?" said Stella, and to Calum, "I expect Hazel's mother or brother'll bring her home."

Calum remained on edge. He kept looking at his watch and when it was seven got up and said he would take a walk along the road. Stella washed the dishes and retired to lie on her bed with a book. She put on a record and thought how pleasant it would be to have her room to herself again. She did not believe that they would ever save up enough money to move. There were Willa and Tom off skiing in the Cairngorms instead of saving that money. Willa had protested at first but Tom had talked her into it, saying he wanted some time with her on his own and she wouldn't have to worry about Betsy as Aunt Ethel was marvellous with small children. He was good at persuasion and prepared to tell the odd white lie to get his way.

When Calum came back he tapped on Stella's door. It was the first time he had ever come to the room to speak to her.

"There's no sign of Betsy. I'm getting worried. I went to a couple of her friends' houses and she wasn't there."

"She knows millions of little girls."

"I know, but the two I spoke to said there was no one called Hazel in their class. Nor in any other they could think of."

Chapter Seven

They went out to search for Betsy, Calum and Stella, and
Felicity and her brother Richard who was fifteen. Felicity
went with Calum and Hamish, and Stella with Richard: it
seemed the best way to split up. Stella was obviously
pleased at the pairing off: she set out with Richard chattering in her high excited way about men who laid in wait for
small girls round the Meadows swing parks. She remembered one from when she was small who had worn a
greasy black jacket and a flat cap and sat staring at all the
girls swinging.

"Should we go down to the swing parks first?"
suggested Calum uneasily.

"If you like," said Felicity. "But it's hardly likely she'd
be there now. If she ever was," she added hastily.

The swings lay idle swaying a little in the wind, the
chute was black and empty. A man came out of the Gents
toilet. Calum looked at him hard. He was wearing an
overcoat and was uninterested in them. Hamish
scampered over the grass, unaware that this was not an
outing for pleasure, and came to heel when called.

They turned away from the Meadows and went up
through the solid respectable tenements of Marchmont

and down into the walled streets of the Grange where houses had gardens of their own and did not share a common back green. Calum carried a piece of paper on which was written a list of names. At each house where they called one name was ticked off and a new one frequently added.

"Caroline's in bed. She's fast asleep, has been for two hours. Wait a minute though and I'll go and waken her."

The mother came back to say that Caroline thought Betsy might be at Lindsay's or Mary's.

"I do hope you find her soon. It must be terribly worrying . . ."

They walked up the road to the next address.

"I expect she'll be in somebody's house, Calum," said Felicity. "She seems to know everyone in the district."

But no one could recall seeing her after school that day.

They returned to the Halls' house where Stella and Richard were drinking hot chocolate in the kitchen and Mrs Hall was saying there was only one thing for it—to phone the police. Stella had stopped chattering.

Two constables came and took down the details: Betsy's age, description, last seen. Calum felt sick as he described her dark red curly hair, snub nose, and green duffel coat. He felt as if she was already dead.

He and Stella walked home with the policeman who proceeded to try to interview Aunt Ethel. They got nowhere of course. Why didn't they go out and start looking, Calum wanted to shout at them, instead of all this writing in notebooks? They had a note of his age, Stella's, and now Aunt Ethel's. Aunt Ethel, with her hand laid over her throat, was declaring that she was going to have a heart attack.

"How was I to know?" she kept moaning.

At last the policemen took their flashlights and went to look. Calum and Hamish accompanied them but Aunt Ethel would not allow Stella to leave the house. She seemed to think that if she let her out of her sight she might never see her again either.

They started on the Cunninghams' street. They went into every passage, going through to the back green where they flashed their lights and Calum called out "Betsy?" as instructed. His voice sounded thin and weak drifting up into the night air. The tenements loomed black and high to the rear, broken here and there by squares of yellow and white light. It was bitter cold: frost was silvering over the grass and the clothes lines glittered.

The door leading into the sixth back green was stuck. One of the constables put his shoulder to it and it jerked open.

"Betsy?" called Calum.

No one answered.

They paraded around the large open space, with Hamish sniffing and the torches lighting the ground in front of them. Someone had left a sheet out. It was frozen solid, like a board. Hamish barked twice in quick succession, strained at his lead. And then they saw her lying in a huddle on the ground beside the wall. Calum reached her first. Her face felt cold as marble.

"Is she dead?" he cried.

"Asleep more likely." The constable lifted her gently up into his arms. "But she's frozen, poor wee mite. Just as well she didn't lie here all night. We'll need a doctor quickly."

Betsy's eyelids flickered and settled again.

They carried her upstairs and laid her, wrapped in a quilt, in front of the fire. A doctor came soon and said he thought they'd better have her taken to hospital.

Calum travelled with her in the ambulance, leaving Stella to telephone his mother and Tom in Aviemore. He felt as if everything was happening in a dream again, the way it had when he first came to Edinburgh. The ambulance swept through the quiet streets, its blue light revolving.

The hospital was quiet too, and warm. Nurses smiled at

him as they passed and told him not to worry and one of them brought him a cup of tea.

"Wouldn't you like to go home?"

He shook his head.

After a while he fell asleep and wakened some three or four hours later to hear his name being spoken urgently. He jerked awake unable to place the cream corridor and strange smells. His mother's face was bending over him. She buried her face against his shoulder. She had been crying.

"She's going to be all right, Calum, thank God! But what a fright I got!"

Tom stood in the corridor, his face grey and drawn. They had had a frantic drive south. The roads had been icy and they had had a bad skid just north of Perth. Luckily there had been nothing coming the other way. They'd come out of it with only a dented bumper and smashed headlight.

They went to see Betsy who was sleeping peacefully with her hands curled round her face. She looked as if nothing at all had happened to her. It took the rest of the family three days to recover.

Betsy was allowed home after being kept under observation for twenty-four hours. She sat in the big chair by the kitchen fire and told her story. Enjoying every minute of it, thought Calum, who still had a crick in his neck from having fallen asleep in such an awkward position on the hospital bench. The car was in the garage being repaired, Aunt Ethel was having treatment for high blood pressure (she was prone to it), and Willa had not been able to sleep since coming home. Tom kept telling her it was ridiculous of her to feel guilty and that no one could watch over children night and day.

Betsy's story was simple: she had gone home with a nine year old girl called Heather after school and stayed to tea, having told Heather's mother that her own mother knew where she was. At seven o'clock Heather had walked her home, leaving her on the corner of the street. On the way along to the flat Betsy had noticed a little white kitten sitting by a door. "It was crying. I had to help it." She had opened the door and followed the kitten in to the passageway. Then it had wanted to go into the back green. So she had opened that door too and gone into the green. And the door had closed behind her. After she had played with the kitten for a few minutes she had tried to open the door but could not. It was stuck. The kitten escaped over the wall and Betsy was trapped inside the back green. Alone, and in the dark.

"I shouted and shouted but nobody heard."

"Why didn't you bang on the door?" asked Tom.

"I did. Nobody came."

Nobody heard anything in the city, thought Calum; they were too busy and too shut away from one another. This would never have happened in Cromarty. If he and the policemen had not found Betsy when they did she would have frozen to death. The thought could be read in her mother's face for a week afterwards.

For the first day or two Tom was also full of concern for Betsy but once she was back to bouncing up and down the corridor with a troupe of small girls he began to voice some of the irritation he had been bottling up.

"She really does do what *she* wants all the time and gets away with it, Willa!"

"Now, Tom, you can't blame her for getting locked inside that back green. It must have been a horrific experience for her."

"It was a horrific experience for a few other people too, not least you! It did happen to spoil our holiday as well."

"So that's what it is! You're more concerned about that—!"

"Nothing of the sort. But when you think of the money—!"

"You're a one to talk about money!"

They then went on to talk about money, heatedly and at

53

length. Calum took Hamish out. It was raining a little but he did not mind that. Anything to get away from the arguing. He had never heard his mother argue so much before. And it was usually about money. A tight frown knitted her brow when the morning post arrived with small brown envelopes. Final reminders. Accounts overdue. Tom would always say he had meant to pay the bill; it had slipped his mind. And it probably had.

Everyone in the house knew that they would never find the money to move, though Willa and Tom still read the property for sale column in the newspapers and drew rings round ones they fancied. It was as if they were playing a game.

Calum managed to get a morning paper round. He wanted to save up for another bike. But apart from that, he enjoyed going out with Hamish in the early mornings when it was still dark and people were sleeping behind drawn curtains. His round included the Halls' street. Often Felicity was up early practising the piano. He could hear the music as he came up the path and would linger a moment on the step taking his time about pushing the paper through.

One morning she opened the door just as he was about to thrust back the letter flap.

"Like a cup of cocoa?"

Wet sleet was falling slantwise across the street.

"Yes please."

They went in to the kitchen fire. His jeans steamed in the heat. Felicity made cocoa and toast and gave Hamish a biscuit.

"I like the way you play," said Calum, surprising himself. At once he felt foolish.

"Oh thank you. Do you know about music?"

He shook his head. He knew nothing at all, only that he liked to listen to some passages more than others.

"Come in any morning you feel like a hot drink," said

54

Felicity when he left. "Just come round to the back door."

But he could never do that. Go round and knock and say, "I'd like a cup of cocoa this morning, thank you very much!" But sometimes she heard him open the gate and would come to the front door, as before. Those mornings came to be the bright ones. On the others he felt disappointment when he had put their paper in and turned away and heard no sound of movement inside. Hamish too looked expectant as they came up the Halls' path. He loved to sit with his paws in the hot grate and have his fur stroked by Felicity.

The weather improved; there were sports after school. Calum was chosen for the Second Fifteen rugby team. He played at half back. His wide shoulders were good in the scrum. They began to win every match they played. He noticed some girls watching when they played a match. Jackie White and Pam Dickson, but never Stella and Felicity. He did not think Felicity would be interested in rugby. She gave a great deal of time to her music—she played the flute as well as the piano—and went to concerts regularly with her family and with Stella.

"You could come with us sometimes if you liked," suggested Felicity but did not make any definite offer, perhaps expecting him to make the next move. His mother used to tell him he held himself back too much.

She used to tell him many more things than she did now, for her time was taken up running a home for five, knitting and weaving as before, and by Tom. They did not argue all the time. Often they laughed and shared secrets; they went to the theatre and out for dinner, usually with Willa protesting that she knew they shouldn't but allowing herself to be persuaded anyway. On those evenings Calum had to look after Betsy who protested that he was like the man who kept the jail as he would not let her out of his sight.

One aspect of Calum's new life that Hamish did not like was his absence in the afternoons and on Saturday mornings. Calum could not take him to the rugby field so often they went late for their walk and had to cut it short to be back for dinner.

"He gets very restless in the afternoons," said Willa. "Sits at the door waiting to get out."

"I can't give up my rugby."

"I wasn't suggesting that you should."

"Oh, maybe I should! It's not fair on Hamish is it?"

"You've got to think of yourself too, Calum."

"If we didn't live in a top flat he could get out when he wanted to."

"Don't start on that again! Please! You know Tom and I are doing all we can."

One Wednesday afternoon they won a particularly important match and won it with a wide margin. Calum played exceptionally well.

"Can I have your autograph?" asked Jackie White afterwards.

He mumbled something in return. He was never sure if girls were trying to get a rise out of him or not. Jackie and Pam went on smiling and chattering. They were all right, he supposed, but he had no idea what to say to them. Felicity was different. He could talk to her because she was quiet and kept still. She was not there to see his triumph of course.

He walked home in good spirits, kicking a pebble in front of him and humming under his breath. He thought it was a tune Felicity played. There was a breath of spring in the air; crocuses were blooming in sheltered spots and one could believe that the trees would bud and sprout leaves again. Afterwards, he could remember every moment of that walk home: the look of the spiky yellow and purple flowers, the smell of the wind, the light in the sky.

"Hamish got out," his mother said the moment he opened the door. She was standing in the hall. "The gas man called to read the meter—"

Calum waited to hear no more. He lifted Hamish's lead

from the hook in the hall.

He ran across the Meadows, calling and whistling as he went. Two dogs played together on an open stretch, prancing and barking. Another streaked alone along a path. None of them was a black and white sheep dog.

From there Calum went to the Queen's Park. It was a large place, covering many acres. His steps slowed. He could not check out the whole area, and besides, dusk was already closing in. He traversed their favourite paths, without success.

He must go home since that was what Hamish was likely to do after he had had his jaunt.

Cars and buses now had their sidelights on; rooms were lit but as yet uncurtained. He walked briskly, scanning every side street, stopping on every corner to look in each direction.

And then he saw Hamish. He was on the other side of the road, trotting along with his tail up and his tongue out as if he had slowed from a long run.

"Hamish!" he cried in relief, and in the next instant could have bitten out his own tongue.

Hamish, normally so good about roads, turned and saw Calum and like an arrow came towards him. A dark red and white double decker bus was coming down the hill filled with people going home from work. The paths of the dog and the bus coincided.

As Calum saw Hamish meet the offside wheel of the bus he felt as if a firework had exploded inside his head.

Chapter Eight

"It's as if someone had died in the house," said Stella.

"Well, it's almost the same thing isn't it?" said Felicity. "I mean, for Calum it must be."

Stella sighed. "Yes, I know." She could hardly bear to look at his face. His eyes had that kind of glazed stare which made you feel he wasn't there half of the time. Which he probably wasn't. And when he went into his boxroom and shut the door she couldn't bear either to imagine how he felt. Tom and Willa talked in falsely bright voices, in an effort to lift Calum out of his depression, and Tom had even gone to the length of offering to get him a puppy. For Tom that was something since he didn't care for the idea of small animals chewing his slippers and leaving puddles all over the floor. But Calum had declined. "No thanks," was all that he'd said. And then Tom and Willa exchanged looks across the table. They were forever exchanging looks. It was maddening.

The only one in the house who was not depressed was Betsy. She had cried when Calum first came home carrying his dog in his arms—they all had—but once they had buried Hamish in Aunt Susie's garden she'd dried her tears and begun to adjust to the idea. She played funerals.

"It's nearly driving me up the wall," said Stella. "Every time I go into the bedroom she's at it."

Betsy had ousted her dolls from their crib and turned it upside down, draped it with a sheet and put a bunch of Willa's dried flowers on top. She intoned bits of the funeral service that she had heard on television. Dust to dust, ashes to ashes . . .

"I wish you'd stop it!" Stella cried when she went home that day.

"Why?" Betsy looked up from the coffin.

"It's morbid."

"What's that?" Betsy rearranged the cloth.

"Gloomy. And it makes me feel ill."

"Mummy says Hamish has gone to Heaven. Do you think he has?"

"How would I know?"

"I'm not sure if he'd like it there. They mightn't have the kind of food he likes."

Stella went behind her screen and sat on the bed from where she did not see Betsy, though could hear her muttering on about dust and dearly beloveds. She opened a book and tried to read. Calum was in the kitchen doing his homework, whilst Willa sewed by the fire and pretended not to watch him. She had been in the middle of giving him a pep talk when Stella came in.

"You've got to get above it, Calum. Oh I know how much he meant to you . . ."

Her father had given her a pep talk yesterday too.

"Can't you try to be friends with him? He needs friends now. More than ever."

She was not sure that he did. And even if her father was right what was she supposed to do about it? They had nothing in common except that her father had happened to marry his mother. Everyone was sorry for Calum at the moment, understandably. She was too, yet a part of her deep down resented all the sympathy he was getting; she knew it and felt mean but could not seem to do anything to change what she felt. At school he was treated like a hero—he played rugby now as if he was a charging bull—and a tragic hero at that. She had never seen him play herself, but Jackie and Pam kept her fully informed. Too fully. Felicity had suggested that they might take him to one of the Scottish National Orchestra concerts on Friday evenings (the Halls had season tickets) but Stella had not thought that a good idea.

Calum found another paper round to do in the afternoons and went jogging round the Meadows in the early evenings and at week-ends, so that outside the house he was in perpetual motion. Inside, he sat like a statue. Stella would have liked to have taken up jogging herself, to keep in training for her ballet, but with Calum in possession of the Meadows, as it were, it was out of the question.

'They stop me doing everything,' she wrote in her diary and underlined 'everything' three times.

Whenever Betsy was mercifully absent, playing in someone else's house, Stella practised her ballet steps and did exercises in her room. And she went to extra lessons. They were preparing for the spring show in which she was to dance the lead in extracts from "Giselle" and "Coppelia." When she was dancing she forgot the MacLeods: she floated away into a different world, a magic world in which she was aware only of the sound of the music and the movement of her body.

And at week-ends she went out to the cottage on the moors to have her ballet costumes fitted. Aunt Susie always made them. Whilst her aunt sewed Stella sat by the window and watched the lambs galloping across the field behind their ungainly mothers.

"It's a pity they have to grow up isn't it?"

Aunt Susie looked up briefly and smiled and then went on sewing. Stella yawned. She felt relaxed. The sight of the lambs and Aunt Susie sewing had that effect on her.

After the ballet show the Easter holidays would begin. Calum was going up to Easter Ross for the two weeks; she would come here, as usual.

"I can come, can't I, Aunt Susie?"

"Come when, dear?"

"For the holidays."

Her aunt took off her thimble and laid the stiff white dress aside.

Stella frowned. "I can, can't I?" A flutter of panic had started up inside her. She had counted on coming. She *must* come.

"I'm afraid not, Stella."

"But why?"

"Uncle Nick and I are going away. I've been meaning to tell you. To America. For three months. He's got a Fellowship and I've got leave of absence from my job. Come on now, don't be so upset, it's only for three months!"

The last three months had seemed like a lifetime; the next, without Aunt Susie to come to, stretched forward into eternity.

'I have nothing to look forward to,' she wrote in her diary. Except the ballet show, she added mentally, but did not put that down. She seldom wrote more than one sentence at a time in her diary. It seemed enough.

Felicity wrote reams and reams, though would not show it to Stella; she kept the book in a locked drawer in her desk. She was more secretive than Stella; she smiled when teased and her cheeks grew pink but she could never be persuaded to tell what she was thinking at those moments.

"Friends don't have secrets from one another," said Stella.

"They can't tell one another everything."

"*I* tell you everything."

She had even told Felicity that she thought her brother Richard was fantastic. She found him easy to talk to: he had the same kind of steady gaze as Felicity, which encouraged you to talk. He listened and commented and

61

asked questions as if he were really interested in her ballet show or Uncle Nick's forthcoming Fellowship in Boston. She never mentioned the MacLeods to him.

She daydreamed about him when she pirouetted round her room, imagined him in the audience, his eyes fixed on her, and at the end when she curtseyed he would applaud and applaud until the sound rang in her ears.

"Why don't your toes get sore?"

Betsy's voice jerked her back into her bedroom, away from that other world, away from Richard. She had not even heard the door opening. Her daydreams were frequently punctuated by Betsy's intruding voice asking stupid questions or making comments of a nature that Tom seemed to find amusing but Stella did not.

"Mummy says I can go to ballet if I want."

"Mummy lets you do anything you want, doesn't she?"

"No. She won't let me eat chewing gum."

"What a poor suffering little girl you are!"

At the table Betsy said, "Stella says I'm poor and suffering."

"We're all poor, Betsy," said Tom and laughed and although Willa smiled she did not seem to find it very funny. "The only one with any money is old Calum there," went on Tom. "He's stashing away all his lolly from his paper rounds, aren't you?"

Calum shrugged and went on eating.

"It's a good thing to save," said Willa quickly. If she thought Tom was attacking either Calum or Betsy she was very quick to take up their defence. Tom seldom bothered to defend Stella. She doubted if he knew when she was being attacked.

"What are you going to do with all that money, Calum?" asked Tom.

"He's going to run away," said Betsy, answering before Calum could, and stilling the room.

"Don't be such an idiot!" Calum's temper rose like a rocket. He pushed away his pudding plate making the table rock and the dishes slide, then he got up and left the room. They heard the front door bang and his feet clattering on the stone stairs.

Interesting, thought Stella.

Willa sighed.

"Kids!" said Tom.

"Would you mind helping with the dishes, Stella?" asked Willa.

"I've got to see Felicity about some homework."

"You can do them before you go," said Tom.

"I'll do them later."

"There's nothing wrong with now," said Tom and departed to the sitting room with Willa. Betsy disappeared.

Stella glared at the strewn table and the heaped pots in the sink. Honestly, family life! You could keep it as far as she was concerned. During the years she had lived alone with her father everyone had felt sorry for her because she had not been part of a proper family.

She *must* go up to Felicity's first; she would do the dishes later. The sitting room door was closed and behind it Tom and Willa were having one of their endless discussions. They did not hear her go.

"Do you really think he's going to run away?" said Felicity. Her wide grey eyes looked troubled.

"He turned scarlet when Betsy said it and then nearly went through the roof. He's got a terrible temper at times. I thought he was going to tip the table over."

In the next room Richard was playing the violin. He was going to be a concert violinist when he grew up. They would tour the leading cities of the world together, he as a famous musician, she as a fêted ballerina.

"I wish he *would* run away," said Stella.

"You shouldn't say that. He must be very unhappy."

"I'll say what I want," said Stella crossly. Everyone was rubbing her up the wrong way that day, even Felicity. There were times when she wished Felicity would lose her temper and shout or scream.

The violin stopped.

"He's very good isn't he?"

"Who? Richard? Not particularly. He just likes playing."

"Isn't he going to be a musician?"

"No, he wants to be a doctor, didn't you know? He's always talking about it."

Felicity and Stella did not have their usual easy intimacy that evening; their talk threatened to dry up. They went downstairs to make coffee.

Richard was drinking a cup at the kitchen table and looking at a Motor Sport magazine.

"Hi, Stella! How's the great world of ballet?"

"All right." Stella knew she was going to blush and could not hold it back. She felt such a fool. Why couldn't she have replied with something witty? If Felicity had not been there in the background with the knowledge that she had, then she might have done.

They joined him at the table and Stella expressed interest in motor racing which she had never given a moment's thought to before. Felicity swirled her coffee inside the cup and gazed into it.

"It's a mug's game," said Richard. "But I find it quite exciting. To watch, that is." He turned his head as the front door bell rang. "I'll get it. Probably be for me anyway."

When he had left the room Stella pulled the magazine across the table so that she could look at it. Some of the cars did look quite amazing. Perhaps they'd go to Grand Prixs together as they toured around the world. Her father had once gone to the Grand Prix in Monaco and written an article about it. "I wouldn't mind going to a race," said Stella. Felicity said nothing.

The door opened and Richard came back with a girl who was in his own year at school, two years above them. She had fine frizzy blond hair and large turquoise eyes.

She wore a soft fuzzy sweater the same colour as her eyes.

"You know Fran, don't you?" Richard said to Stella.

Stella knew Fran but Fran did not know her.

On the way down the road black fury raged in Stella's heart. She could have killed Felicity. Why hadn't she told her Richard was going out with Fran Petersen? It had been quite obvious from the way she greeted Felicity and walked round the kitchen that she had been there dozens of times before.

Betsy was in bed, Calum's door was shut, and Tom and Willa were in the kitchen. He was washing the dishes, she was drying and putting away.

Tom turned round when Stella came in. His eyes were blazing.

"Why the hell didn't you wash the dishes when you were told to? You don't do a bloody thing to pull your weight in this house."

"I was going to do them when I came back." Stella's anger matched his. Why couldn't she have done them when she came in? "If you want to do them yourself that's your lookout."

His hand came out; she did not duck in time. He caught her a sharp blow on the edge of the cheek. They stared at one another for a moment. He had seldom struck her.

"I hate you! And *her*! And I don't want to live here any more."

She turned and ran from the room, from the flat, from them. She went bounding down the stairs taking two, three and even four at a time. The door opened above and her father's voice called after her.

"Stella, come back here! At once!"

She went on. She felt capable of flying.

On the last flight her foot turned as she landed, she tried to grab the stair rail but missed. Her left ankle twisted outward and she tumbled down the remaining steps.

Her father took her to hospital. The pain in her foot was agonising: it shot in every direction if she made the slightest move. She sat in a wheel chair in the Out Patients department with her leg supported by a strut that came out from beneath the seat. Her foot was swelling up and already turning a variety of colours.

"Bonny looking sight eh?" said Tom.

"Not bad."

"What a clot!" He squeezed her hand.

Although her foot was on fire with pain she felt strangely at peace. Tom fetched her a cup of coffee and some magazines but she didn't want to read. She watched the night life of the Casualty Department going on around her thinking that one day Richard Hall might be working here. The sister said she was sorry they might have to wait a while as they were frantically busy; they'd had several emergency cases in the past hour. Much more urgent cases than Stella's foot. One man had fallen on barbed wire, another two had been fighting, and another involved in a road accident.

"Not the most cheerful place to spend the night," said Tom.

The small grey waiting room was hot and thick with cigarette smoke. Two women sat chain smoking and staring into space. Tom was smoking too though he'd been trying to give up recently. Willa couldn't stand the smell of cigarette smoke in the house. Most of Tom's friends smoked like chimneys.

After an hour Stella and Tom moved through to the consulting area which was divided into sections by screens. They could hear someone groaning on the other side of the curtain which was splotched with brown stains. Dried blood, thought Stella.

"I wouldn't recommend you to do this *too* often," said Tom.

After another long wait a young doctor pushed aside the curtain and asked cheerfully what she'd been up to. He thought Stella might have broken her ankle; he sent them to X-Ray. They waited again. And again, once the foot had been X-Rayed, to get the results. Stella's toes were turning purple. She wanted to massage them but could not bear to touch them.

They were almost asleep when they were called back to see the young doctor who informed them that there was nothing broken. It was a case of torn ligaments, and the remedy was rest. She would have to keep her foot up for at least two weeks and would be supplied with a pair of crutches.

"In five or six weeks you should be almost back to normal again. In the meantime you'll have to play hopscotch."

He put a crêpe bandage on her ankle and sent her off to be fitted with a pair of crutches.

Willa was still up when they arrived back at two o'clock in the morning. She fussed over Stella helping her to undress and get into bed. She put a pillow at the end of the bed for Stella to support her foot against. Betsy woke up and began to cry and was told very sharply to be quiet and go back to sleep.

Stella slept until the middle of the morning, not wakening even when Betsy got up to go to school. Sun was flooding the room.

Willa brought her breakfast in bed and whilst Stella ate it Tom sat on the chair beside the bed and chatted to her.

"Aren't you lucky? You'll be able to read heaps of lovely books. I could be doing with a couple of weeks in bed myself. Oh, and Felicity phoned to say she'd be round after school. And so would Jackie and Pam and about half a dozen others whose names I can't remember. So you'll be able to hold court!"

He took away the tray. She lay back with her arms pillowed behind her head. Her foot was throbbing but apart from that she felt all right.

And then, suddenly, she thought of something which had not occurred to her before. She would not be able to dance in the ballet show! But she must be able to! She *must*.

She looked at the calendar and counted the days. Ten. There was no chance that she would be able to dance by then. The doctor had said it would be five or six weeks before she was *almost* back to normal. She closed her eyes and felt hot tears pricking against the lids. She heard Aunt Ethel's voice inside her head. Her great-aunt had a habit of saying things that came to you at the wrong moments.

"I don't believe in accidents. Folk bring things on themselves."

It would be a different story of course if she was to have an accident herself.

She came to visit Stella in the early afternoon.

"What a to do eh? You'll need to watch that ankle or it might never be the same again." She managed to fit herself into the bedside chair. It creaked and the sides bulged. "Seems to be one thing after the other. I don't know! Those MacLeods have brought nothing but bad luck into the house, if you ask me."

Chapter Nine

As he travelled north Calum felt his spirits lift, in spite of everything. In spite of one thing, mostly.

He felt as if he had lost a limb: he was incomplete. When he jogged across the Meadows or walked up the street he kept looking behind involuntarily, expecting to see the black and white face and the pink tongue lolling.

"Don't look back!" his mother had told him.

He was trying not to, but it was difficult. In his head, as he ran, he repeated the words, letting them keep time with his steps. Mornings were difficult too, wakening, remembering.

Every time he saw a dark red and white bus he remembered.

And bound up with this grief was the blame that he had for himself. If he had not called Hamish's name . . .

"One can't think like that, Calum!" said his mother. "Ifs and buts can go on for ever."

Or back. If one went back far enough one could say that if they hadn't come to live in the city Hamish might never have been killed. He had said it. His mother had not such a ready answer to that one. After a while she had said that after one took a course of action one must follow through without questioning what might have happened if one had not. Was she thinking more of herself than of Hamish when she said that? Did she think she had made a mistake in marrying Tom Cunningham but wouldn't let herself admit it?

"It's Calum MacLeod, isn't it?"

He looked up to see a Cromarty man standing in the aisle. He used to be a fisherman but worked on the oil now, on a rig in the North Sea.

"How're you liking Edinburgh then?"

They talked of that, and of Calum's father, and of the oil.

And then the question came. "Hamish with you?"

Calum took a deep breath and answered. It would be the first of many times that he would have to answer the question.

"I'm sorry lad. That's tough."

The train took Calum as far as Inverness where he caught a bus to Kessock Ferry. As the ferry boat carried him across the narrow stretch of water to the Black Isle his excitement mounted. He kept his eyes on the cool quiet land ahead. And when his feet touched the ground on the other side he smiled.

Another bus would transport him on the last part of his journey to Cromarty. He found a seat at the window and a moment later a woman who had known his mother squashed into the place beside him. Her lap was heaped high with shopping baskets and carrier bags which spilled over on to his knees. She talked for the whole of the ten miles. Through the window he watched the thin silvery trunks of birch trees flicker past, and clumps of dark green fir, and then large sweeps of land unbroken by any trees at all. The woman's voice lulled him, as did the sight of the green grass and blue and white sky. By the time they came down the hill into Cromarty itself he felt half-asleep as if in a trance.

His old friend Andy Nicol was waiting for him. He

70

reached out and took one of Calum's holdalls.

"Hi, Calum!"

"Hi, Andy!"

That was all they needed to say; they moved off side by side and it was as if Calum had never been away at all. He had written to Andy about Hamish so that not even that question had to be asked and answered.

Every turn in the road was familiar, every cottage, every face. So different from the city where he passed hundreds of people who did not even look at him.

As they walked through the town, Calum was struck by the colours of the houses. Most were washed white or cream but their doors and window surrounds were painted brilliant red, egg yellow, bright blue and pale blue, pink, mauve, raspberry, green. It was as if he was seeing them for the first time.

"The colours are grand aren't they?" he said to Andy, who seemed surprised at this remark. "And I like the way the cottages are put down down all higgledy-piggledy and not in neat rows. In Edinburgh the houses are made of grey stone and set out in straight lines."

"I thought Edinburgh was supposed to be a fine city?"

"Oh it is. Very fine. And very beautiful."

It was beautiful in a different way from this, he reflected, as they trudged on out of the town along the country road. Both were all right, each in their own way. He knew which one he preferred.

Mrs Nicol was in her warm kitchen baking bread. Willa used to say she was one of the most wholesome women she had ever known.

"It's lovely to see you again, lad."

"Mum sends her love."

"What a pity she couldn't have come too!"

Calum nodded and they gathered round the table.

Mr Nicol came in from the fields. They had home made soup followed by stew which was thick with vegetables from the croft and with it they ate lots of fresh warm bread.

There was little talk whilst they ate. No one argued. The three months in Edinburgh dropped away from Calum and became unimportant. It was as though he had been on a long journey and returned home. This *was* home.

And it was where he was going to stay, though probably not with the Nicols, for he couldn't expect them to take him in. They only had three small rooms and their croft barely supported them. Every now and then Mr Nicol went off to work for a spell on the oil himself.

That night Calum slept without nightmares for the first time for three weeks and wakened in the early morning to see the sun coming through the thin curtain and the shadow of a hen stalking across the ceiling. He lay on his back and smiled. If only Hamish—

He stopped himself and got up at once.

"You're up early." Andy's nose poked above the coverlet.

Calum did not want to waste a minute.

He went out into the cool morning and sniffed the wind. It ruffled his hair and stung his cheeks. He could see for miles across the Moray Firth to the North Sea. Mr Nicol was glad to have a hand with the milking. He had six cows, all black and white Friesians. They discussed the milk yield and milk prices and the state of farming in general. The life was hard, Calum did not need Mr Nicol to tell him that; he knew that they survived from one season to the next and hoped nothing drastic would happen. Storm, flood or unexpected frost could change their fortune overnight.

"And how's the school work going, lad?" asked Mr Nicol.

"All right."

Calum did not tell him about his thoughts on becoming a marine biologist. It was still very much an idea that floated around in his head, and not something to be announced.

"I'm hoping Andy'll stay on at school. I'd like to see

72

him get a good job. This kind of life won't do for him."

Calum was not sure how Andy felt about the future: they never spoke of "what they would do when they grew up." It was a subject you got to write about in school essays. The only person he had ever discussed the topic with was Felicity. It was strange to think of her here, so far away from the city, and its streets and problems. He sat back, patted the cow's flank, inhaled the smell of manure and warm milk. He could imagine her here. He could imagine walking with her across a field to meet the sky. He felt sorry that he would not see her again. Perhaps he should write to her. But he knew that he would not, for what could he say? And after a month or two she would have forgotten him.

Now Stella he could not imagine in this place at all. She would disturb the peace.

He forgot about them both and went to drag Andy from his bed.

They went fishing that day, from the harbour pier, and for most days after it, and when old Angus was going out in his boat they went with him. From the harbour Calum looked across Cromarty Firth at the oil fabricating yards in Nigg Bay. He watched the giant cranes moving against the sky and stared at the huge drilling platform under construction and imagined his father like an ant crawling over it.

Calum was to stay for a week with the Nicols, then move round the coast to where his father was encamped with his new family, some twenty miles from Nigg Bay. They lived a bit like gipsies. It was a life he wouldn't mind himself.

The days of the week slipped by and it was as if he had never been away. To begin with everyone said, "Nice to see you back, Calum," but after that they greeted him as if he had never been away.

For the first day or two he avoided their old house down by the waterfront. And then one day he went alone to look at it. The new people had given the walls a fresh coat of whitewash. It was a stout little cottage, low, with windows looking across the Firth, its door set in the side street away from the sweep of the wind.

It's only a house, he said to himself, and went on his way, though inside it was not what he felt. After he had passed it a few times the ache lessened. Everything passes in time, said his mother. Sometimes that was a comforting thought, at other times not.

He bought two coloured postcards. One was of the house where Hugh Miller had been born and bred—he had been an eminent geologist in the nineteenth century and Cromarty's most famous son—and this he sent to his mother. 'Mrs Willa Cunningham,' he wrote, and still found it odd that this should be his mother. The other postcard showed the cottages along the shoreline against a bright blue sky. He had thought he might send it to Felicity. He carried it in his anorak pocket till it became bent and wrinkled.

His last evening with the Nicols arrived. In the morning his father was coming to collect him.

"Now you know you can come and stay any time, Calum," said Mrs Nicol.

He thanked her.

"Will you be back in the summer, do you think, lad?" asked Mr Nicol.

Calum nodded.

"Time's not long in going," said Mrs Nicol.

That night Calum lay awake after Andy had gone to sleep and thought about his father. He was a bit like Tom Cunningham, he supposed, in that he paid little attention to the past or future. At least he gave no sign that he did. Tom would *talk* about the future and make promises and when he didn't keep them he was downcast. His father would never promise anything. You had to take him or leave him as he was.

Calum sat on the dyke at the road end waiting. His

74

father had set no time for coming, in the letter had put, 'Expect me when you see me.'

Around mid-morning he arrived driving an expensive new estate car splashed half-way up its sides with mud. He jumped out to greet Calum. He was a big brown-haired man with wide shoulders. Calum took his build from him.

"It's great to see you, lad! You're looking well too. Edinburgh must be agreeing with you."

He went striding down the track to see the Nicols and they responded to his cheerfulness. Normally quiet and fairly reserved, they opened to him like flowers unfolding in the sun, and after he left they would say, "He's not a bad chap, Dave MacLeod. He's full of life. A pity he and Willa weren't able to make a go of it together."

It only took half an hour to drive round the coast. Dave MacLeod drove fast but skilfully, handling the long car as if he had had it for a year rather than a week. They talked about cars on the journey, and the oil construction industry. Dave MacLeod enjoyed his work. He worked hard, was highly paid and had good spells off to enjoy the money. The life might have been made for him.

"And how's the young madam?"

"She seems okay."

"Tell your mother to send her up with you next time."

His mother hated having messages sent from his father via him. She would become pompous. "You can tell him if he wishes to communicate with me he should do so by letter."

"I'm sorry about Hamish, Calum," said his father. "I'll get you another dog if you'd like one. It'd be the best thing for you, you know."

"I couldn't have another one, not in the town, Dad. Not in that flat."

"Ah well, maybe when they move."

"I don't think they'll ever move."

His father made no comment on that. He never did

when Calum said anything about Tom or Stella or the life in Edinburgh.

They turned into the field where a number of oilmen and their families had set up an encampment. Their large caravans, shiny with chromium, were known as 'superior living homes,' a far cry from the old gipsy type van. They were equipped with electricity and all had television sets.

Three women were gathered outside one caravan.

"Forever blethering!" said Dave MacLeod and tooted his horn at them. "Women!"

When he made remarks like that in front of Willa her hackles would rise.

The women waved back.

They wore skirts and high-heeled shoes which Calum always wondered at. It seemed a place more for jeans and Wellington boots.

The estate car bounced down the muddy track to the MacLeods' home.

Linette came to the door with the baby on her hip. Her blond hair fell in waves to her shoulders. She wore trousers, tight blue velvet ones, and spiky-heeled shoes. She was twenty-five years old, fifteen years younger than his father.

She was pleased to see him: she said so and gave him a hug and kissed his cheek. She smelled of a mixture of perfumes.

Inside the van you might have thought you were in a bungalow. The feeling of spaciousness surprised Calum every time he arrived to stay. And everything was spick and span: the formica surfaces shone, the cushions and curtains were startlingly clean, a vase of daffodils sat on the table, and nothing lay around. You had to be tidy when you lived in a van, Linette said. Calum did not mind tidiness: he found it natural to clear away something when he had finished with it, or to put a book back on the shelf. Everyone else in the Edinburgh flat—his mother included —was untidy. Books, magazines, balls of wool, carrier

76

bags, all added to the immovable clutter. "I'm just a natural born slut," his mother often said cheerfully.

In that way she and Tom were suited.

Gary, who was two, and Shirley ten months, were amazingly well-behaved. The baby lay on a cushion and kicked her legs and gurgled and the little boy played with plastic bricks in a corner. Linette said that the children had to be well-behaved when you lived in a van, otherwise life would be impossible. Calum shuddered at the idea of Betsy confined to a few feet. Her visits here were never successful.

They had steaks for dinner that night and a bottle of red wine, followed by another. "You only live once," said his father. "Give the cat another canary!" It was warm and cosy round the table looking out into the night. The other vans made blurs of light against the black field and through uncurtained windows could be seen the flicker of television sets.

They watched television too once Linette had cleared away, and Calum fell asleep during the late night film.

His father had the week off. Some days they stayed around the site watching television, reading, playing cards or football; others, they took the car and drove off up the coast, going as far as John O'Groats one day, and across to the west coast fishing port of Ullapool on another. Whenever they went for a drive they ate out, usually in expensive restaurants. His father hated picnics. Sitting on damp grass, eating gritty sandwiches, trying to stop papers flying away in the wind and having kids knock juice over the travelling rug was not his idea of fun. Nor Linette's either. They were well suited in this way.

Sometimes his father went to the pub with the other men on the site and then Linette would make coffee and sit down to have a chat.

"I'm really glad of your company, Calum. It's a pity you're not nearer the way you used to be and could come more often. It's all right when your Dad's at home, like this week, but when he's working I feel like climbing the wall at times. And there's not much wall to climb is there?"

"I thought you liked living here?"

"*Like* it? Come on, Calum! Who'd want to live in a caravan in the middle of a muddy field when they could be living in a house on a proper street? You should try it on a wet winter's night. Or even a dry summer's night for that matter! I feel so restless at times."

If he were to come and live with them he could babysit and then they would get out more often. And when his father worked on a Sunday he would be company for Linette. There were two bedrooms, one for his father and Linette, the other for the children. He could sleep in the sitting room area, as he was doing now. The seats converted into two single beds, and during the day bedclothes and pillows were stored underneath out of sight. He would not clutter the place up and Linette knew he was tidy. And he could go to the local school.

He had thought it all out and come to the conclusion that it was quite feasible.

Two days before he was due to return to Edinburgh he put the idea to his father. They had gone for a long walk together and his father had been saying how pleased he was that Calum and Linette got on so well together.

"She's real fond of you, son. Enjoys having you around."

It was then that Calum made his suggestion.

His father stopped dead.

"You're not being serious are you?"

"Why not, Dad? I hate living in Edinburgh and you've just said Linette likes having me—"

"That's a bit different from having you to stay in the van all the time. If we had a proper house then it might be different. But as it is, it's just not on, son."

Chapter Ten

By the start of the summer term Stella was able to walk again without crutches, though could still only wear gym shoes and had to take her time, especially when going up and down stairs. But at least gym shoes were an improvement over one shoe and one sock. She exercised her foot daily, as she had been instructed, and wished it would hurry up and mend. The tennis season had begun.

She sat on the edge of the court on the Meadows and watched Felicity and Pam playing singles and limped to fetch the ball when it rolled within easy reach.

Aunt Susie and Uncle Nick were in Boston now. Their key hung on a hook in the Cunninghams' hall. Stella had gone with her father to check the house after they left. It had had an empty, closed up feel, even after so short a time. They might never come back: they might like Boston so much they would decide to stay, or go on somewhere else.

"Susie always did want to travel," Tom had said as he relocked the door.

The ball bouncing close to Stella's left foot brought her back to the grey asphalt court and the call of voices. She caught the ball neatly against her chest, surprising herself.

Raising her arm, she threw it in a wide arc to Felicity and enjoyed even that small bit of activity. Sitting on the sidelines did not suit her.

Calum jogged past in his navy blue and white track suit. When he drew level, he lifted his head to indicate that he saw them. He had had a good holiday, it seemed, not that he had told her anything about it. Willa had questioned him at length, asking about this person and that, and how had the old place looked. As if it would be looking any different from when she had last seen it! Calum made the Black Isle sound like the garden of Eden, whereas Tom had told Stella it was a fairly windswept place on the edge of the North Sea. She would never go there herself.

Felicity won the set. She was a strong, confident player; Pam scuttled about like a hare dodging from one side of the road to another in front of a car. They came to talk to Stella and get their breath back. They would play only one more set, they promised, and then they'd be ready to leave. Stella said she would go round the corner and buy Coke and crisps. They delved in their anorak pockets and found enough money amongst them. Stella was thinking of getting a paper round herself: she was fed up being short of money. Before Willa had come into their lives Tom used to slip her extra ten and fifty pence pieces and had not expected her to manage on her bare allowance.

Money continued to be a problem in the Cunningham/MacLeod household. Tom had been low in work recently —that was how it was when one freelanced—and Willa was trying to increase her knitting output. Stella hated the clank of the knitting machine.

The Pakistani shop was busy: people were buying milk and rolls, bunches of pale orange tulips, sweets, cigarettes. Two of the customers were girls from Stella's class; she stood by the crisp stand with them and chatted until the owner came by with a stack of wire baskets and moved them on. They stood outside to finish the conversation. They talked about everything, and nothing very much. A clock chimed somewhere.

"I'd better go," said one of the girls. "My mother's waiting for these eggs."

Stella drifted slowly back towards the tennis courts. It was as if time itself had slowed in the past month. She walked when before she would have run, idled when she would have hurried along. Other people seemed to be moving too fast; they overtook her and reached the end of the street by the time she was half-way along.

When the courts came into sight she stopped abruptly. She frowned, shaded her eyes with her hand against the lowering sun, wondering if she was seeing correctly. She was.

She went a little closer, inching her way along, making no sound, not wishing to be seen or heard. Not that they could possibly hear the soft fall of her gym shoes on grass. Pam squatted at the side of the court with her back to Stella, watching the players. And out on the asphalt, playing, were Felicity and Calum.

Calum had said he didn't play tennis but he appeared to be doing well enough. He moved with speed and agility defending his territory and he had great strength in his forearms, so that whenever his racket met the ball square on it drove it back across the net with tremendous force. Sometimes he failed to make contact—due to lack of practice and experience obviously—and then he would shake his head and laugh. He was actually laughing! Out loud. And so was Felicity.

Stella put the Coke bottle down beside her feet.

"Fifteen love," called Pam.

Stella turned and walked away, running almost. Her foot had miraculously refound some of its old strength, though lost it again on the first few steps back up to the flat. It took her ten minutes to climb the three flights. At the top she remembered the bottle of Coke.

Willa and Tom were in the kitchen discussing flats. The newspaper was open at the property page and Willa held a red Biro poised over it. They did not notice that she was limping painfully. She collapsed into one of the armchairs.

"We've been to see a flat, Stella!" said Tom.

"Oh?"

"And we think it's a distinct possibility."

She sat up. "You mean you're thinking of *buying* it?"

"Well, you'd all have to come and see it first of course," said Willa. "And then we'd need to talk it over."

"Where is it?"

"Not far away," said Tom, and Stella knew by the tone of his voice that he was giving the good news first and the bad would come later.

The flat was at Tollcross, which was not far away, but the street was drab and grey and had no views of the Castle or Arthur's Seat. It was lined with tenements on both sides.

"But there *are* six rooms," said Tom. "It's the only way we're going to get more space. We can't have everything."

"Yes, we must be realistic," said Willa and smiled.

Stella hated being realistic. And she hated people smiling when she felt like screaming. She skirted Betsy who was having a pink plastic tea party in the bedroom and stood by the window looking out over the open green sweep of the Meadows. Who wanted to stare at a row of ugly old flats opposite if they could have this instead? But with this came Betsy and her high chiming voice. At least in another flat she would have a room to herself again. Neither of course was the right solution.

Three figures were coming across the Meadows, three that she recognised. She watched as they grew larger and could make out their faces. Calum was walking between the two girls who wore their cardigans slung around their necks as they had seen Wimbledon players do on television and they swung their rackets in their outside hands. They were all talking and laughing and Pam and Felicity kept turning in to look at Calum who was in the middle. Stella closed the curtains.

They went to view the flat at Tollcross. It was another top floor flat, three flights up.

"It'll keep us fit," said Tom cheerfully, as they moved up the dank stone staircase towards the light. He was determined to be cheerful, which Stella found exasperating.

The flat had previously been occupied by an elderly woman who had just died. The place smelt of death. Dark stains blotched the wallpaper obliterating roses and violets; the woodwork was the colour of treacle; water dripped from ancient taps into discoloured sinks.

"A lick of paint and it'll look quite different," said Tom.

"Yes, don't be put off by the decoration," said Willa. "And a good scrub will soon get rid of the smell."

They walked around silently, gazing at the walls, the windows, the view across the street.

"I don't like it," said Betsy.

"Shush!" said Willa, and eyed the estate agent who was showing them around.

"It's a very good property," said the agent. "All the cornices are intact, you'll notice. And the chimneys work. Coal fires are making a big come back."

Two rooms were up a small narrow stair: these were the rooms which Tom and Willa thought would be suitable for Stella and Calum. They trudged up the steps, one behind the other.

The rooms had sloping ceilings and dormer windows that gave a view of the roof-tops across the street, and the sky.

"Quite spacious aren't they?" said Tom.

"Not bad," admitted Stella grudgingly.

"I want this room," said Betsy, standing on her toes to look out of the window.

The one earmarked for her was the smallest in the flat.

"You are going to sleep downstairs beside us," said Willa.

"*Are* we going to buy it then?" asked Stella.

"No, no, we haven't decided yet, but if we do—"

A bell tolled somewhere below. It was the old-fashioned kind of bell worked by a brass pull.

"Excuse me," said the estate agent. "That'll be the next viewers. I'm just about run off my feet. There are so many people after the place."

He went clattering down the stairs whistling.

"They always say that," said Tom. "To make you feel keen."

How could anyone be *keen* about a place that looked like this one? Stella wondered. Unless of course you were desperate. Were they?

Willa said she thought they should go home and talk it over.

She made hot chocolate—Tom had a beer saying he needed something stronger to cope with such a momentous decision—and they all sat around the kitchen table.

"Now then," said Willa brightly, "let's hear what you think!"

"I don't want to go," said Betsy.

"You'll do what you're told!"

"That's not fair."

"Life's not fair."

"Calum?" Tom looked at him inquiringly.

"I'd be for it, I'd like a bigger room."

"Of course you would! It's not as if you have a proper room at all at the moment. What about you, Stella? Don't you think you'd like that big room with the sloping ceiling? It could look very nice painted white."

For a moment she had been thinking she might quite like it; now she felt herself shifting away from that position. "I'd miss the view from my window here."

"Oh, we'll all miss something, love."

"I know, but I've always had that view."

Willa was silent, but thinking plenty, one could see that.

"Willa and Calum had a view of the sea in Cromarty,"

said Tom.

"Then they should have stayed there," said Stella, and left the room.

Tom followed her down the corridor into her bedroom.

"Why the hell do you always have to be so damned unpleasant? Just when we were all getting together and trying to come to a decision!"

"To do what *you* want. And Willa."

"We shall go ahead and try for the flat whether you like it or not. If you behave like Betsy then we'll just have to treat you like her."

"I won't go with you, unless you drag me there."

"And where else do you think you could go?"

"Aunt Ethel's. She said last week I could come and stay with her if I wanted to."

"O.K. then, go and stay with Aunt Ethel and see how you like that!"

He banged the door behind him.

She lay face downward on her bed. She hated him and everybody else. And that included Felicity.

Chapter Eleven

They decided to go ahead and buy the flat.

"Do you think you should if Stella doesn't like it?" Calum said to his mother.

"Tom says she'll calm down and come round to it. You know they both tend to over-react to things." Willa smiled. "And they don't mean every little thing they say when they're wound up."

A surveyor was hired to survey the flat. He reported that it needed to be rewired and replumbed—which they could have told him—but, apart from that, the fabric was sound. And the Building Society agreed to lend.

Then came the agonising part of trying to decide what figure to offer. Tom wanted to go three thousand pounds over the starting price, Willa one. They had a week in which to decide before the closing date for offers.

"I didn't know that was how you bought houses," said Calum. He was having a cup of coffee in the Halls' kitchen during his afternoon paper round. "It seems funny to bid and not know what anyone else is offering."

"It's a terrible system we have here in Scotland," agreed Mrs Hall, who was making dough for bread. "You can end up offering for five or six houses before you get one. And that means five or six surveyors' fees."

"I don't think we could afford *too* many of those."

"Perhaps it'll be a case of first time lucky," said Felicity.

"Perhaps." Calum was trying not to let his hopes rise too much, though it was difficult not to. As Tom said, you had to think about the flat as if you were going to get it, so already they were choosing colours and planning which furniture they would move into what room. All but Stella who kept up a stiff-faced silence. Sometimes Calum thought she was on the brink of saying something when she would check herself and close her mouth firmly.

"Haven't seen Stella lately," said Mrs Hall. "Is she all right Calum?"

"Think so," said Calum, and felt uncomfortable.

"You'll need to tell her not to neglect us."

Mrs Hall put a cloth over the dough and left it to rise.

After she had gone Calum and Felicity were quiet. They drank their coffee and stared at the scrubbed wooden table and Calum thought he heard Felicity sigh. She was thinking of Stella too, he could sense it.

"Calum—"

"Yes?"

"Stella—well, I don't think she likes us being friends."

"No, I don't think she does."

Felicity sighed, quite clearly this time.

"Maybe I should stop coming?"

Felicity had her head propped between her hands and her elbows on the table. The fall of straight brown hair hid her face. She did not move.

Calum got up and lifted the newspaper satchel from the floor. She looked up at him and her wide grey eyes were unhappy.

"Maybe you'd better, Calum. For a while."

When you stopped doing something it wasn't often you went back to it, thought Calum, as he walked down the path and out of the gate. That had been his experience anyway.

The following morning he pushed the Halls' paper through the letter flap and turned away quickly. Felicity was not playing the piano.

When he passed her in the corridor at school they exchanged little half-smiles but when Felicity was with Stella they passed without any sign of recognition. He saw her around with Stella again in school and hanging about outside the shops, though she stayed away from the Cunninghams' flat. Stella was going to the Halls once more.

"You fallen out with Felicity?" asked Pam, to whose house he also delivered a paper.

"Don't be silly." Calum felt his face becoming warm. Was that what Felicity was saying?

Pam would have liked to have discussed it further but he said that he would have to be getting a move on since he was late as it was. Tonight they were to decide on their offer for the flat.

"You've got to be bold in this game," said Tom. "It's the only way to get a look in."

But Willa was more cautious and mindful of the amount they would have to pay monthly for the mortgage.

"There were lots of people looking at it," said Calum and stopped, wondering if his mother would think he was taking Tom's side.

"Looking," said Willa. "Doesn't mean they'll offer."

"I don't like my room," said Betsy. "I want one upstairs."

"*You* can go to bed!"

Betsy went, under protest, returning at intervals until Willa threatened to cut off her Saturday pocket money.

The amount to be offered was debated for another couple of hours. Stella was supposed to be writing an essay but her concentration was not on it; Calum gave up all pretence of doing homework. Willa and Tom did numerous sums on pieces of paper, working out the cost of removal, rewiring, redecorating, all of which they had done before. At the end of it they were back where they had begun, with Tom in favour of offering two thousand pounds more than Willa.

"Let's sleep on it," said Willa.

At breakfast she filled the border round the newspaper with more calculations. Tom yawned over a cup of coffee. He was not a morning man.

"I think we should keep our offer down," said Willa, as if she had just come to that decision. "After all the place *does* need a lot doing to it."

"You're probably right."

Offers closed at noon. All morning in school Calum kept thinking about it and wondering if by the time he went home at lunch time they would have acquired a new flat. Soon he might be able to unpack his boxes, put his books on shelves, set up a work bench.

He ran home when the lunch bell sounded.

Willa and Tom were pacing the sitting room floor, in so far as it was possible to pace between a knitting machine, a loom, a piano, and too many pieces of furniture.

"Maybe we should have gone a bit higher, Tom."

"You always think that when you're waiting. I have the feeling it's going to be all right."

The door opened, in came Stella. She was breathless. "Well?" she demanded.

"We're waiting for the lawyer to phone."

The telephone sat on its table looking as if it would never ring again. Suddenly, life erupted from it. Tom seized the receiver before it got out its second ring.

"Tom Cunningham here." They watched his face and knew at once what the outcome was.

"Oh well," said Willa. "There'll be other flats." She looked tired.

Tom replaced the receiver. He told them the amount of the winning bid. It was exactly fifty pounds less than what he had wanted to offer.

"You see, I should have listened to you, Tom," said

Willa. "I was far too cautious."

"Don't go blaming yourself now, love. It's all a gamble."

After the excitement, the swinging to and fro of their expectations, the anti-climax was difficult to cope with and a kind of lethargy descended on the household. Willa half-heartedly circled a few ads but Tom said they should wait a day or two before starting on the whole palaver again. He began going back to the pub in the late afternoon and coming home after they had eaten their evening meal, often bringing Mungo or Bill. To avoid a slanging match, thought Calum. There was nothing very mysterious about Tom.

The light May evenings made Calum restless. And the boxroom felt more and more like a box, an imprisoning one, airless, sunless, cheerless. At times he wanted to stretch out his arms and push back the walls. Instead, he went down into the Meadows.

He drifted across to the area of the tennis courts and swing park, not running or jogging, but taking his time, letting himself enjoy the smell of the grass and the sight of the blue and white puffy sky. Windows flashed golden in the sunshine.

He no longer looked back, though every time he walked across a stretch of grass he still missed Hamish. A small terrier came up to him snuffling at his legs and he stopped to pat his head. He made a point of looking at dogs. In the first few weeks after Hamish had died he had always glanced away.

The tennis courts were busy: all were full and a knot of people waited to get on. Stella would not be there for she had gone to visit her Aunt Ethel. Calum loitered to watch for a few minutes before moving on.

The swing park, in contrast, was almost empty. Only one swing was moving a little, as if disturbed by a breeze. On it sat Felicity, her feet lightly grazing the ground, her hands loosely holding the chains that suspended the seat from the overhead bar. She did not notice him until he sat down on the next swing. The chains creaked and she lifted her head.

"Hi," he said.

"Hi," she said.

He began to swing, very gently in the first instance, and as he did she began to move too, so that they swung backwards and forwards, to and fro, in unison. Gradually, they went higher, but not too high, for they did not want to rock the frame. The swings were meant for children younger than they. The ground dropped away below them and they sailed up into the summer sky. Calum watched Felicity as he leaned back making his body work the swing. She was pink-cheeked and smiling and her long thick hair floated free in the bright air. The sounds of traffic and people came as if from a long way away.

And then the arc of their swinging grew smaller and smaller and they moved more and more slowly, as they came back down towards the earth. Their feet touched the ground, scuffed it a few times, stopped. They got up and left the swings.

"Would you like a Coke?" asked Calum, who had not known that he was going to put the question before it was out.

"Wouldn't mind."

He took her to a café at Tollcross that sold ice cream, soft drinks and coffee. They found a vacant table by the wall.

"What would you like then?" asked Calum. "You could have a milk shake with ice cream if you want."

"I haven't got any money, Calum."

"I've got plenty." He jingled a few coins in his pocket and grinned. "Well, enough."

They both had coffee-flavoured milk shakes. They sat opposite one another and drank them through straws, elbows on the table.

"It's gorgeous," said Felicity, pausing when the level

on the glass dropped to half-way. She sighed but it was not the kind of sigh she had made the last time they had been on their own together, in her kitchen, when they had been thinking of Stella. He put all thoughts of Stella from his head now.

"How're you getting on with saving for your bike?" asked Felicity.

"All right. I should be able to get it for the summer holidays."

"That's good. Will you go back up north?"

"Yes."

"For the whole summer?"

"It depends."

It depended on many things but he did not want to think of them at this moment. He just wanted to drink coffee-flavoured milk shake and watch Felicity's face as she drank hers. Their eyes met and held and he felt a little rush of excitement. He had not imagined that he could look into a girl's face as he was doing now, without feeling awkward and wanting to look away.

She looked away first. She dropped her mouth to pick up the straw again. She drained her glass.

"Like another?"

"Another?"

He laughed at the expression in her eyes.

They had chocolate flavour this time. She giggled a little as they began to drink.

"You'll be making me drunk."

"On milk shakes?"

That made him laugh too. They took a long time to finish the second drinks and for long moments forgot about them altogether. Outside, the slow summer dusk was creeping in.

"Gosh, look at the time!" said Felicity. "It's gone half-past nine. Mum'll be wondering where I am."

He walked her home without saying that he would. When they turned off the main road he took her hand in his. It felt warm and soft. He rubbed his thumb along her palm. They walked slowly so that they would not reach her house too quickly.

Ten struck on the church clock. They hesitated on the corner of her street.

"I'd better go," she whispered. "I'm terribly late."

He bent his head and kissed her mouth. It too felt soft and warm, and sweet.

Whirling round, she left him and went running off up the street. He touched his mouth with the back of his hand. He did not remember walking home.

Chapter Twelve

One minute Stella quite favoured the idea of moving to a new flat, the next she wanted to stay on in the old one. She was torn. About a lot of things.

When Betsy was at her most irritating Stella was all for moving: then she felt she couldn't stand living like this for another day and would do anything and go anywhere to get a room of her own. Even Siberia. In fact, at times Siberia looked quite inviting. But when Tom and Willa rowed she thought how awful it would be if they were to sell and then the MacLeods departed. For it was still a possibility that they would. Aunt Ethel said she couldn't see it lasting. Leopards didn't change their spots that easily. If at all. She knew Tom. And in her opinion he wasn't a marrying man. He *had* married twice, which would seem to suggest that her opinion wasn't very astute, but Stella did not point that out.

On Willa's birthday they had a real dust up. Tom forgot to come home until ten o'clock. He met an old friend who was just back from Australia and whom he hadn't seen for five years. They met in a pub of course. Where else? And they had a lot to talk about. Five years was a long time.

The five hours that Tom was out seemed like a long time too.

Willa cooked a special meal and put on a new summer dress. She carried Tom's typewriter and papers into the bedroom and laid the table in the sitting room window with the best cutlery, tall green candles and green paper serviettes to match.

"You won't be late, will you?" she said to Tom before he went out.

By half past six she was looking at her watch, and at seven chewing the edge of her lip. She stood in front of the window with her arms folded scanning the paths that crossed the Meadows. Even Betsy knew to be quiet; she slid into the kitchen and helped herself to a lump of cheese. Calum sat in the kitchen with a book in front of him.

At eight o'clock, Willa called out, "Come on, everybody, let's eat! I expect Tom'll be in soon."

They ate in the sitting room and Willa lit the candles but it was not what could be called a festive meal. Willa tried to be cheerful and made a joke about Tom and his drinking buddies but no one laughed. The food was good though so they ate that, all except Willa herself who pushed the food around on her plate and kept glancing at her watch.

They finished the meal and there was still no sign of Tom. They carried the dishes through to the kitchen going along the corridor in silent Indian file.

"I'll wash up," offered Stella, who felt she could afford to be generous.

"It's all right." Willa's voice was sharp. "I'll do it myself." She jerked on the tap and water bounced off the plates in the sink spraying the front of her new dress. "Damn! This is the last straw!" She turned to face Stella and Calum. "How could he do this tonight of all nights? How *could* he?"

"Tom's bad," said Betsy.

"Go to bed, Betsy. At once!"

She went without complaining. Stella had been about to slip away to her bedroom too but now couldn't since she didn't want to have to comment on the shortcomings of her father to Betsy. She knew that it was a shortcoming of his to treat people in this way. But that was what he was like and you just had to take him as he was. It was beginning to look like Willa would not take him as he was for very much longer. She was swishing the water round in the sink and slapping the dishes on to the drying rack with a ferocity that Stella had never seen in her before. The storm when it broke would be very fierce.

Tom arrived with a bunch of flowers and declared himself to be an absolute heel. He wasn't going to attempt to defend himself, he said, he knew he was in the wrong and he hadn't meant to stay so long but he and Jack had had so much to talk about and then Mungo had come in. . . Willa waited till he ran down.

"Didn't mean to," said Willa. "That's what the kids say."

Then she threw the flowers across the room.

"Look, Willa, I do understand how you feel—"

"Go to bed, Stella and Calum."

Betsy was lying with the bedclothes pulled over her head. Stella lifted the corner and folded it back.

"You can't do that. You might suffocate."

Betsy's eyes peered over the top of the sheet. "Are they going to have a fight? Will they hit one another?"

"Of course not!"

"I'm not going to ask Tom to my birthday party."

He's not a bad man, he's not, Stella said to herself as she lay in the darkened room; he's good and he's kind and he makes me laugh and he's my father and I love him. Exhausted, she fell asleep.

The next day Tom apologised to all of them. "I'm very sorry I spoiled your evening. I'm going to take you out for a Chinese meal tonight to make up for it. And I'm never going to be late again!"

"I'm not asking for the moon," said Willa.

"Why not? You deserve it."

So they had made it up. But would they if it happened again? Stella had overheard Willa saying to Tom that she was at the end of her tether. Willa's tether seemed to stretch like a piece of elastic. Her own, she felt, might easily snap.

Stella stood in the hall in front of Aunt Susie's key wishing that her aunt and uncle would come home again. In the last letter they had said they were going on an extended vacation across to the West Coast before returning. After that they might sail across the Pacific Ocean to Australia. Well, it *was* possible. And after that they might never be heard of again.

Stella glanced around. She was alone in the flat. There was no sound of feet on the stairs outside. Stretching out her hand she slid the key off its hook. She held it in the palm of her hand for a moment as if weighing it.

Then, quickly she went to her room and closed the door. She wrapped the key in a piece of cloth and put it at the back of her bottom drawer, under the striped sweater that Willa had made for her. She closed the drawer. She felt her heart beating faster.

The key was not missed for several days. When Tom said, "Anyone seen Aunt Susie's key?" no one had.

"Are you sure you haven't touched it, Betsy?" asked Willa. "You weren't playing at houses by any chance?"

"I haven't touched it. I haven't!"

"All right! I wasn't saying you had."

"Doesn't matter," said Tom. "They've got a spare key at the farm."

It comforted Stella to know that she had the key in case she needed it. Since the row on Willa's birthday Tom had stopped going to the pub by himself. If he showed signs of being restless in the late afternoon Willa would say, "Hang on a minute, I'll just put the dinner in the oven and we can go out and have a drink together." They would come back in half an hour. And sometimes Willa invited his friends for a meal. The kitchen came to be full of people eating spaghetti or moussaka and drinking red wine on Saturday evenings. Bill and Mungo kissed Willa fondly on arrival and departure and said things like, "Good old Tom, you always did have an eye for a bonny woman!"

And they resumed house hunting.

Of the next five flats they looked at three were disgusting and two possible. One was a mile or so away and would mean rather a long walk to school for Betsy. Willa thought it would be a nuisance to have to take Betsy to and from school every day. "Stella or Calum can do that," said Tom. But Stella did not fancy having to walk Betsy to and from school every day either. She said she wouldn't always be able to as some days she had tennis and others canoeing, and Calum said he had his paper rounds. They dithered so long the flat was sold over their heads to a man who put in a quick offer.

"We'll need to be quicker off our marks next time," said Tom.

Stella snorted.

"And what's that meant to mean, madam?"

"Nothing."

They worked up an enthusiasm for the fifth flat, which comprised a ground floor and basement, and within twenty-four hours had notified their lawyer and called a surveyor. The survey showed extensive dry rot, wood worm and wet rot in the basement.

"I'm beginning to think I must be blind," said Willa. "I've lost all faith in my own judgment."

"I don't believe we'll ever move," said Stella.

"I thought you didn't want to?" said Tom.

"Depends. On what we move to."

Now if the Halls had been buying a house all would have gone smoothly. They would have made up their minds, chosen wisely, without arguing or swithering, and got a bargain.

Stella did not see so much of Felicity out of school these days. Felicity was preparing for her music exam at the end of June: she practised morning and evening. Richard was working for his O Grades, Mrs Hall was swotting for an A level in Greek just because she liked to 'stretch herself,' and Mr Hall was trying to finish a thesis. He would too, Stella was sure of that. The Halls were what Tom called 'achievement orientated.' Nothing wrong with that, he added; he wasn't sneering. "Tom could do so much if he only applied himself," said Aunt Ethel.

On light evenings Betsy found it even more difficult to settle down in bed.

"I'm afraid I'll have to draw the curtains, Stella," said Willa apologetically. "Otherwise she'll be awake till midnight. You can go into the sitting room, love. Tom and I are playing Scrabble in the kitchen."

But Stella did not feel like sitting in the sitting room alone. She decided to go and see Felicity.

"She's up in her room," said Richard, who opened the door. "How're you? Haven't seen you for ages."

"I'm fine." She could not seem to find much more to say and, besides, probably Fran Petersen would be in the kitchen drinking coffee, and listening. The door was ajar.

Felicity was lying on her bed listening to a pop record. She looked startled when Stella came in. It used to be that they popped in and out of one another's houses all the time. But recently things had changed between them; they were less easy together. Felicity got up from her bed and began to move about, shifting things from one place to the other. She was not usually so fidgety.

"Got new jeans?" asked Stella.

"Yes."

"You didn't tell me."

"Must have forgot."

She was wearing a new shirt too, a striped one, in

varying shades of pink and grey, and a pink band held back her newly brushed hair.

"Going out?"

Felicity nodded. She turned her head away and her hair hid her face. "I've got to go and see my music teacher for a few minutes."

Stella walked up the road with her and they parted on the corner.

"See you in the morning!"

Stella went to Pam's house. Her father came to the door carrying a newspaper and with his glasses pushed back from his forehead.

"She's out, dear. Goodness knows where she is! I'd be the last person to know."

Stella continued on up to Jackie's. Her mother said she had gone to play tennis with Pam.

After that, Stella did not feel like calling on anyone else. She did not feel like going home either. Walking briskly, as if she was meeting someone and was late, she set off for the Queen's Park.

Inside the park people wandered in twos or else in groups of three or more. A man and a dog passed. A clump of boys called and whistled after her and she hastened on, her cheeks burning and annoyed with herself because they were. Stupid idiots! If she had been with Felicity they would have laughed.

She left the path and climbed the hill. Half-way up she stopped to rest and get her breath back. The city was spread beneath and around her, its spires, towers and chimneys standing against the sky. She hugged her knees and felt less alone in some curious way.

And then, she saw Felicity and Calum. They sat, as she did, on a grassy knoll looking over the city; they were a little below and to the right and so could not see her. They must not have seen her when she was climbing up either.

She was wrong about one thing: they were not looking at the view, but at one another.

Chapter Thirteen

As soon as Calum read the letter from his father he shoved it back into its envelope crushing the paper.

"Any news?" asked his mother idly. She was trying to decide what kind of meat to buy for the week-end.

"No, not really." He put the piece of bacon into his mouth and found it difficult to swallow. He had been looking forward to his breakfast—on Saturdays and Sundays they had something cooked—but the letter had killed his appetite. He struggled through the food so that Willa would not ask if there was anything wrong with him.

Stella excused herself and left the table. She had a ballet lesson. Tom was still in bed, and Betsy had already gone out to play. She rose before seven on these fresh summer mornings.

"Dad said maybe I'd like to go up next week-end," said Calum.

"And would you?"

"Wouldn't mind." He would have to go, whether he minded or not. "He's sent a postal order for my fare."

"Well then you might as well go, mightn't you? Especially as it's a long week-end. I suppose you *could* take Betsy with you. She hasn't seen her father for ages."

"I don't think that would be a good idea," said Calum hastily.

"She should go sometime."

"They've got some plans for the week-end." Calum was vague. He lifted the letter and pushed back his chair.

Willa let him go and returned to writing her shopping list on the back of an old bill.

In the boxroom Calum took the letter from the envelope and read it again, more slowly this time, so as to make sure he had got the correct message.

His father had written to say that Linette had left him, taking the children with her. 'When I came home from work yesterday she had gone. She left a note saying she couldn't stand the life any longer. I saw it coming a while ago.'

Calum had not seen it coming, had never imagined the van without Linette and her bright blond hair and the two small children chattering and playing, although in the past he had wished for it. Fervently. How odd that often things one wanted very much came at the wrong time, after one had ceased to want them.

He went to talk it over with Felicity.

"I never took it seriously when Linette went on about being lonely. All the women grumbled."

But Felicity was more interested in what Willa might do rather than Linette, as was Calum himself.

"You don't think your mother would go back to him, do you?"

"I don't know. I used to hope she would."

"But you don't now?"

He shook his head.

They were sitting on a rug in the Halls' garden. The sun, unusually hot for May, was beating down on them which made him, whose skin burned easily, feel hot and a little uncomfortable. Felicity, however, was turning a nice shade of brown. The gean and lilac trees were in full blossom; their scent filled the air. Bees swayed over the flowers.

102

"Do you think she'd want to go?"

"I don't know."

What was troubling him was the thought that she might, and it was for that reason that he had not told her about Linette. Things were always swinging up and down between her and Tom: one minute they would be laughing and the next arguing. And they had made no progress with house hunting, yet they all knew that they could not go on living so cramped up for ever. "You can't settle in to a place until you unpack *everything*," said Willa every time the topic came up for discussion.

"There wouldn't be room for you all in that caravan though would there?" said Felicity.

Calum had already thought of that, but his father might be able to rent a house for them somewhere in the area. He earned enough money.

"Why didn't he rent one for Linette?"

Calum did not know the answer to that either. As far as he could remember Linette had liked the idea of living in a van in the beginning. She used to make jokes about being a gipsy and a wanderer but they had not done much wandering, unless you counted driving up and down the coast in a fast car.

"Do you want to go under the shade?" asked Felicity. "Your nose is beginning to burn." She wrinkled her own at him.

They dragged the rug under the gean tree and Felicity fetched home-made lemonade from the kitchen, and two pieces of warm sticky gingerbread, newly baked. They spent a lot of time in the garden, he and Felicity, even when the weather was dull or rainy. Then they sat inside the Wendy house that her father had built for her when she was small. It was quite a large hut, with a window and a door that closed and enough space for two to sit comfortably on cushions. Calum liked it when rain fell thick and straight, hammering on the roof, drenching the green garden outside, and they sat inside close and warm

103

together. He liked sitting under the gean tree with Felicity too, watching the sunlight flickering across her face. The high stone wall surrounding the garden kept it and them private.

They knew full well why they wanted to be private though they never discussed it. They each knew what the other was thinking much of the time. Though not all of course. That was scarcely possible. But it was the first time Calum had felt like this with another person. With Andy he was at ease, they didn't have to talk if they didn't want to, but it never occurred to Calum to wonder what was going on in Andy's head.

He did not allow himself to imagine what was going on in Stella's head. She seldom spoke to him directly, she might make a remark that he was intended to hear, but that was the limit of their communication. She had become 'bosom pals', as Willa called it, with Pam and Jackie. The three girls whispered in corners and burst into loud, seemingly uncontrollable laughter when he appeared. They spurned Felicity also, though greeted her with silence, not laughter. Felicity said she didn't mind though Calum wondered if she did underneath. Her cheeks flamed to a deep rose colour whenever the three friends passed by, arms linked, their eyes ready to look back and stare.

"Aren't you friendly with Felicity any more?" Tom asked one day at the table.

"No. I'm not." Stella looked directly at Calum. "She's a nasty little sneak."

"A sneak? Felicity?" Tom laughed.

"Oh you think she's just perfect don't you? Because she plays the piano and she's always top of the class and all the teachers think she's marvellous! Little Goody Two Shoes!" Stella swept from the room like a tornado.

Tom looked after her. "What was all that about?"

"Oh, you know what kids are like," said Willa. "Always falling in and out with one another."

"Do you fall in and out with people, Calum?" asked Tom.

"Calum's best friends with Felicity," said Betsy.

Willa and Tom turned together to look at Calum. He held their gaze without dropping his. So it was true: Felicity was his best friend. For a moment there was silence around the table. Betsy swung her legs and grinned, pleased at having caused a sensation.

"Oh well," said Tom.

Later Willa came to Calum's room. She was frowning.

"I know I probably shouldn't interfere," she began.

"Then don't!" he said, quite roughly. He felt rough. And defiant. And guilty. He felt so many different things that he was unable to separate them all out.

"Don't speak to me like that, Calum!"

"You said you shouldn't interfere."

"I don't like the idea that you've taken Felicity away from Stella—"

"I haven't *taken* her away! What do you think I am?"

Willa sighed. She had nothing more to say.

Lying awake listening to the creakings and rustlings of the flat as it settled down for the night, Calum wished that he could take Felicity away with him when he went north next day. They could live like gipsies—she wouldn't be like Linette who got bored with the sea and the wide open sky—and roam around Scotland, going where they pleased. And that would not include Edinburgh.

Calum's father met the train in Inverness. He was on time. Before driving on up the coast they went to a steak-house overlooking the river and had a steak and salad. During the meal his father did not mention Linette; he asked whether Calum was liking the Edinburgh school any better now and how was Betsy? Calum answered guardedly. He felt guarded, was apprehensive as to what question his father might put next. And yet he was glad to be back with him again. They got on well together: there was no denying that.

It was still light when they arrived at the encampment. Some of the men were sitting on the steps of their vans smoking and drinking beer. A woman unpegged the last of her washing and walked off carrying the basket against her hip. She lifted her free hand to wave to Calum.

The trees were full and thick, the grass long and luxurious.

"It's not a bad place to live," said Dave MacLeod. "You feel really close to the earth here."

Calum nodded.

"I've never been much for houses myself. What about you, son?"

Calum was saved from having to answer by the MacLeods' next door neighbour opening her window to call out.

"Nice seeing you again, Calum."

"Thanks."

They were probably all watching from their windows.

"Folk have been very decent. We all help one another out when it's needed."

His father unlocked the van and they went inside. It seemed very empty, like a classroom after hours. It had the feeling of a place where no one had ever lived. Not a trace of Linette or the children remained.

"Well, make yourself at home! You can have your usual bunk."

Calum unpacked his bag and his father had a drink seated by the window looking out over the camp.

"Anything special you'd like to do tomorrow? We could go over to Cromarty if you'd like?"

They went after breakfast. Andy did not seem all that surprised to see them. He just said, "Want to go fishing?" and Dave MacLeod said he'd leave them to it. He spent the day calling on old cronies and drinking with them in the pubs.

Calum and Andy fished from the harbour. They did not

speak any more than they usually did though all the time Calum's thoughts were racing this way and that, a bit like a fish in disturbed waters.

When they were eating their lunch he said, "Linette's gone off and left Dad."

"Isn't she coming back?"

"He doesn't think so."

"Mum said he'd have his hands full with that one."

"Oh?"

"Well, with her being that much younger." Andy pointed across the Firth. "Look, there's Angus!" They did not speak again of Linette that day.

Dave MacLeod did not speak about her either. Calum supposed there was not much more to say now that she had gone. But his father's face had changed: at times there was a tight hurt look in it that Calum had never seen before. Even when he laughed he looked as if he had been punched between the eyes.

On Sunday morning his father slept late. Calum got up early and went for a long walk. Few people were about, birds chirped in the tree-tops, gulls swooped low over the water. In spite of the arrival of the oil and all the upheaval that went with it, this was still a quiet land. One could hear the birds rather than the rumble of traffic.

In Felicity's garden you could hear the birds too. He sat on a boulder and skimmed stones through the waves, watching them plop and rise and create little ripples of foam of their own. Two swans were pecking amongst a clump of seaweed further along. He thought about Felicity and then he thought about his father and that hurt lost look in his face. After that he gave up thinking; he concentrated on the stones and the shimmering sea and the call of the sea birds.

They spent the day around the camp site. They put chairs on the grass outside the van and sat in the sun. Dave MacLeod read through a large pile of Sunday papers, after which he went to sleep; Calum read 'The

Catcher in the Rye,' which Felicity had lent him. Her name was on the flysheet: Felicity M. Hall. The M stood for Mary. He knew so many little things about her: what her favourite colour was, her favourite food, and drink, and books, and music. He knew she loved milk shakes.

"Good book, Calum?" The woman from next door called across.

"Yes." He must have been smiling. He lifted the book and began to read. "Everybody reads 'Catcher in the Rye,'" Stella had said scornfully when she saw him carrying it. Everybody presumably meant her too.

His father cooked the evening meal. The pork chops spluttered and caught fire and filled the van with acrid smoke which stung their eyes and made them cough. They opened the door and windows.

"I'm not much of a cook, I'm afraid," said Dave MacLeod, spearing one frazzled chop with a fork and holding it aloft. "Let's go and buy fish and chips!"

They had to drive twenty miles to buy them. His father would drive any distance to get anything he wanted. It was whilst they were sitting in the car eating the fish and chips that he brought up the subject that had been lying on his mind all week-end.

Chapter Fourteen

Willa got a letter from Dave MacLeod on the Saturday
morning that Calum was away. Stella, who was sitting
opposite, watched her face change as she read. When
Willa reached the end of the second page she remained
motionless for a time staring into space. She had forgotten
Stella. She got up and went to look for Tom. He was in the
bathroom.

"I'm just coming through," he called.

He came in his dressing gown.

"I've had a letter, Tom." Willa glanced at Stella. Stella
ate a piece of toast and pretended not to be interested.
"It's from Dave," said Willa in a rush. "His wife's left
him."

"Come to her senses eh?"

"It's not funny, Tom."

"Sorry, love, don't suppose it is. But it's got nothing to
do with you any more, has it?"

"No, not really."

"You sound as if you think it might have?"

"It's not me—it's Calum."

"Shouldn't you be off tripping the light fantastic,
Stella?" said Tom.

"There's no ballet today because of the holiday weekend."

"Well, go and buy a pint of milk then."

"We don't need milk."

"We always need milk. Go!"

She took her time and Willa was unable to wait until she had quite left the room.

"Dave wants Calum to go and live with him, Tom."

"Would he want to?"

"I don't know. He might. He loves the country so much and he's fond of his father."

"You wouldn't want him to go though, would you?"

"Of course not! I'd miss him." Willa sighed. "But I couldn't stop him if he wanted to. He's old enough now to make up his own mind."

Stella's heart was hammering with excitement as she went down the stairs. If she had not had to be so careful with her foot she would have leapt down two, three or four steps at a time.

The first person she saw in the shop was Felicity. She was buying rolls.

"Hi!" said Stella.

"Hello, Stella." Felicity was quick to answer.

"Hang on a minute! I've just got to get a pint of milk."

Felicity waited outside the door, the bag of rolls clutched against her chest. Stella joined her. They began to walk along the road.

"I'd like to be friends again, Felicity."

"Oh, so would I, Stella!"

"Especially now that Calum will be going away."

"Going away," Felicity frowned. "How do you mean?"

"Back to Easter Ross of course. Didn't he tell you? His stepmother's gone and left his father so the plan is that he'll live with him. Makes sense really. Well, Calum's always hated Edinburgh and we're so squashed up we're like sardines."

"Are you sure?"

110

"Willa had a letter this morning."

He's bound to go, he's bound to! thought Stella. She was not telling a lie. And it did all make sense. Calum could live in the middle of a field with his father and get another dog and go fishing when he wanted to and they would be left in peace down here. Each to his own, Aunt Ethel liked to say.

Stella turned up Felicity's street and went with her as far as the Halls' gate. Felicity did not ask her to come in for a cup of coffee.

"I'll see you," she said in a small voice and walked off up the path, head held very straight. Stella knew she would go up to her room and cry.

Stella went home and wrote in her diary.

'O.K., so I'm mean. I was mean to Felicity. But I couldn't help it. And she asked for it. *She asked for it.*'

She underlined the last sentence and stared at the words until they started to jiggle and dance before her eyes. They did not make her feel any better. She pushed the diary into the back of a drawer. As she was about to close it she remembered Aunt Susie's key. She checked that it was still there and felt comforted.

Willa and Tom were in the kitchen, in the same positions she had left them in.

"I suppose I'll just need to get used to it, Tom," Willa was saying. "All kids go away sometime."

Stella put the pint of milk on the table.

"Thanks," said Willa, without looking.

"We're going to view a flat this afternoon, Stella," said Tom. "Want to come?"

"No thanks."

She lay on her bed all afternoon watching the sky through the window. She did not want to read or go out. There was nothing that she felt like doing and no one she felt like seeing. If only Aunt Susie was at home! But Aunt Susie had not even written for three weeks.

Tom and Willa went to view the flat and came home

111

enthusiastic. They resumed their financial calculations. The kitchen table was covered with pieces of paper and old envelopes by dinner time.

"We've decided to offer," said Tom.

"Good," said Stella, who did not care one way or the other.

It was one of the longest week-ends she had ever spent. Pam was away and when Jackie rang up to see if she was coming out she said she didn't feel well.

"Are you all right?" asked Willa. Willa laid a hand on Stella's forehead. "Temperature seems normal. But maybe you'd better go and lie down."

Betsy, dressed in a nurse's outfit, brought pretend medicine in the pink plastic tea-set. Stella opened her mouth obediently, swallowed unidentifiable liquids and let Betsy chatter on without protesting. "Just you lie still like a good girl. . . ." Perhaps she would become seriously and interestingly ill. She might go into a decline as girls did long ago when they were unhappy in love. Then Tom and Willa might stop talking about flats and mortgages and telephone bills for ten minutes and Aunt Susie might fly back from America to be at her bedside.

"Open your mouth now. Wide!"

Betsy put a pencil on Stella's tongue and peered into her throat.

"Don't like the look of that. Better have some cough sweets."

Betsy prescribed Smarties. Stella sucked them slowly as instructed, letting the flavours of chocolate and orange dissolve on her tongue. It was odd but she found it soothing to have Betsy fussing round her. She even felt slightly hypnotised.

But by Monday morning she had had enough of playing patient and was restless again. Betsy stamped her foot and said she was not to get up. She did.

Tom and Willa were trying to decide if the curtains would fit the new flat and if not how much it would cost to replace them.

On the Meadows people lay on the grass, some with their sleeves rolled up, a few in bikinis, trying to acquire a tan. Stella lay on her stomach and stared into the short dry grass. She watched a ladybird climb on to the back of her hand and hike up her forearm. At the elbow it dropped off, falling on its back, quickly righting itself to continue on its uninteresting way. But perhaps it was not uninteresting for the ladybird.

Two feet in baseball boots had stopped in front of her nose. Letting her eyes travel up a long pair of jean covered legs she saw that they belonged to Richard Hall. At once she scrambled to her feet, brushing stalks of grass from her front.

"Thought it was you." He said one or two things about the day and the weather and holidays and then, "Why don't you go up and see Felicity? She's mooning about the garden looking as if someone's trodden on her tail."

Richard went away after a little while. Stella watched him until he dwindled into a small moving speck and then vanished. She stayed on the Meadows all day, close to their flat, so that she could run for cover if she wanted to. Why she would want to she was not sure, but she felt that she might.

Willa and Tom made a diversion to speak to her on their way to see the flat again. Tom was carrying a measuring tape.

"Come with us, Stella," he said. "It'll give you something to do."

"I don't want to."

Tom and Willa exchanged one of those infuriating looks. They were worried about her, thought it unhealthy to hang about all day on your own doing absolutely nothing.

On their way back they came and sat beside her on the grass. Willa's bare legs were very pale. Freckles were flowering on her arms and nose.

"We've decided to go ahead and offer," said Tom. "The flat's really roomy and it's got an open view over the side of the Meadows."

She hated their cheerfulness. It made her feel more and more as a tortoise must when retreating into its shell.

"You can choose new curtains for your room, Stella," said Willa.

"*If* we get the place."

"We've got to be lucky sometime," said Tom.

"I don't see why."

"What *is* wrong with you anyway?" demanded Tom and got up without waiting for an answer.

In the evening Calum returned from the North. They had been waiting for this moment, all but Betsy who was unaware of what was going on. Nothing conclusive could be read from Calum's face. He looked subdued, but then he was seldom to be seen leaping about or grinning openly. Except when he was with Felicity.

Why had he ever had to come here? thought Stella fiercely. She hoped he would be going away very very soon.

Calum and Willa shut themselves up in the sitting room for an hour and talked. Stella stayed in the kitchen with her father who was writing an article on the decline of the country school. He kept asking her opinion but she had none. Hadn't she spent her whole life in the city? That didn't mean she shouldn't think about other places, he said.

He looked at her over the top of his typewriter. "What is eating you?"

"I'm just fed up, that's all. Don't you ever get fed up?"

"I have been known to."

"Well then."

Her father knew better than to recommend some silly therapy, like knitting, as Willa might. Her hands were seldom still.

"You'll feel better when we move. We all will. We need

114

to make a fresh start. It's a mistake to stay on in a place that has other associations."

He was trying to talk to her on a level, one adult to another. She did not respond.

"The first few months were bound to be difficult, Stella. Until we got the creases ironed out."

He talked as if he thought they *were* ironed out.

He went back to battering his typewriter. He worked at ferocious speed making numerous mistakes, his hands unable to keep up with his thoughts. Willa often said it sounded like machine gun fire.

Stella heard her footsteps in the passage. She held her breath. Willa was smiling.

"He wants to stay with us, Tom!"

"Great!" Tom jumped up and seized her hands in his. "I'm really pleased, Willa."

They did not notice Stella leaving the room. Betsy was fast asleep surrounded by a dozen plastic dolls of varying sizes and hair colours but all wearing the same doltish expression. Stella tiptoed past her bed to her own one. She switched on her lamp and sat for a few minutes in the yellow glow without moving.

Then she took her diary from the drawer and wrote in it, 'I shall *have* to do something now.' She underlined 'have.' Before she went to sleep she made sure once more that Aunt Susie's key was where she had left it.

Chapter Fifteen

The week following his return from the North was a difficult one for Calum: he kept thinking about his father, imagined him sitting alone in the van smoking and drinking too much, looking out across the field at the other families. The encampment was a place for families.

"You're not going to change your mind, are you, Calum?" said Felicity.

"No."

"Good."

"Don't you want me to go away?" he asked teasingly, knowing the answer already. Felicity wrinkled her nose at him.

Taking the decision had been hard: he had been torn and at first confused. His first impulse had been to say yes when his father asked him. The issue, for a moment, seemed simple. His father wanted him to live with him. His father needed him. And his mother didn't, not in the way that she used to. She had Tom now.

Calum had sat in the caravan trying to sort out his feelings which tugged him this way and that. He wanted to live in Easter Ross again, yet he wanted to go back to Edinburgh too. He wanted to go fishing with Andy and he wanted to go on seeing Felicity. He wanted to be with his father but he also wanted to be with Willa. His thoughts had revolved like a spinning top until he felt dizzy. He had had to stop them for a while and go for a walk until he could think things through a little more calmly.

His home was with Willa: she had brought him up. That was the conclusion he came to. And to stay with her and Betsy was what he wanted to do more than anything else, for the present.

His father had not blamed him. "Why should you want to come and stay with me? I walked out on you, didn't I?"

"It isn't because of that."

"Must be partly. Stands to reason. Not to worry though, I'll survive, I daresay. And I'll come down to Edinburgh to visit you. I won't want to spend my free time sitting around this field."

"He's bound to be lonely in the beginning," said Calum to Felicity. Light rain was falling, not much more than a fine spray known as Edinburgh mist. They sat in the Wendy house with the door open as the day was warm and close.

"Do you think you need to worry so much about him? I mean, he *did* leave you and Betsy after all. And your mother. She must have had a bad time."

"You think he's selfish, don't you?"

"A bit," said Felicity, obviously meaning a lot. "Don't you?"

"Yes, I suppose I do. But he's my father."

"Don't look so sad," said Felicity. She touched his face.

He put his arm round her and she let her head rest against his shoulder. A cat jumped from the garden wall disturbing a bush of Christmas roses. Water spilled from the leaves.

"Stella wanted to hurt me," said Felicity. "That was why she said you were going away."

"We've hurt her, haven't we?"

"You mustn't sigh like that. You sound like an old

117

man."

"All right!" He laughed. "I won't sigh any more. But what *are* we going to do about Stella? We'll have to do something."

His mother had had a talk with him. "How would you feel if Andy went off with Stella and ignored you?"

He had found that difficult to answer since he couldn't imagine Andy going anywhere with Stella. And yet how could he tell? But he didn't think he'd mind as much as Stella minded about him and Felicity.

"Maybe that's because Stella's friendship with Felicity was different," said Willa. "They virtually lived in one another's pockets."

But he had agreed that things could not go on as they were.

"You will have to leave time for Stella to be with Felicity," said Willa.

That meant he wouldn't be able to spend as much time with Felicity as he had been doing.

Willa thought that might not be such a bad thing. "You could play cricket again. And there's that nice boy Daniel you know at school. You might go out with him sometime. Or what about some of the boys in the rugby team? You mustn't cut yourself off from other people."

She did not want him to be alone too much with Felicity, or too often. She said they were too young to become too intense about one another. Mrs Hall also thought so. They could tell that from the number of times she came into the garden on flimsy excuses. To look for a trowel. To hang out a wet towel in the rain. To ask if they'd seen her shears.

"Why can't people leave us alone?" said Felicity.

"Because they're there, I suppose."

That made Felicity laugh. He felt her laughter flowing into his own body. If only they could stay in the Wendy house for ever!

"Are you two not going to come inside and have some

118

tea?" They had not heard Mrs Hall approach on the wet grass. She was bending down to look in at them. Her face looked funny and lop-sided. "I've baked some scones. And a cherry cake."

She watched them over the rim of her cup as they drank their tea, noticed every time they looked at one another. People are trying to separate us, thought Calum, as he took a piece of cherry cake from the plate which Felicity's mother held out. She asked if he was going north for the summer. She asked in a disinterested sort of way but he knew underneath she was very interested.

"I don't know. It depends. On whether we get this flat or not."

If they did he would have to help with the removal. Offers closed at noon the next day.

At breakfast-time they were still debating what to offer. It could go on and on like this for ever, thought Calum wearily. He did not bother to come back in the middle of the day to find out the result.

They got the flat. Their offer topped three others.

"I can't believe it," said Willa.

"Neither can I," said Tom. Both sounded stunned.

They made no move to start working out removal costs.

"I suppose we'll have to get some estimates," said Willa.

"Let's leave that till tomorrow. I'm going to take you out to celebrate this evening!"

"Me too," said Betsy.

"No, not you too. Your mother and I are going out on our own."

"You can all have chicken and chips for supper," said Willa.

Calum took Betsy with him to buy them. She loved going to the chip shop. She pressed her nose against the glass counter and examined the golden-brown pieces of fish and chicken and spring rolls waiting to be scooped up and eaten.

"Hello, sunshine!" The man behind the counter winked at her as he shook salt on the chips. "Lots of sauce eh?"

As they opened the flat door Stella came from the bedroom looking slightly odd. Yes, there was definitely something strange about her, Calum decided. She seemed excited. Her cheeks were flushed and her dark eyes bright. She gave most of her chips to Betsy who declared she was going to burst but continued to eat until she had finished every last crumb.

Stella put her chip paper into the pedal bin and left the kitchen.

"Bed for you," said Calum.

"Not yet," said Betsy.

"Yes! Mum said."

"Ten minutes."

He gave her twenty and then she went without too much fuss. He suspected she had a pain in her stomach from the chips, though would not admit it.

Stella was in the bedroom behind the screen. Calum saw her shadow when he went to check that Betsy was all right. He returned to the kitchen to clear up.

Shortly afterwards Stella put her head round the door. "I'm going out for a while."

He did not know why that should make him feel uneasy but it did. She never did tell him where she was going of course so there was no reason why she should have done this evening. He shrugged. What she did was none of his business. He switched on the radio.

But he could not get Stella out of his mind. He rang up Felicity.

"Stella hasn't come up to see you by any chance?"

"No. Why should she? I mean, she doesn't come up to see me any more."

"No particular reason."

They chatted for a few minutes and then Mrs Hall

wanted to use the 'phone so Felicity had to ring off.

He dialled Pam's number. Her mother said she had gone to play tennis with Jackie.

"You don't know if Stella's with them do you?"

"Oh I couldn't say, Calum. She could be though."

In the bedroom Betsy lay asleep, sprawled on her tummy. Stella's tennis racket stood propped against the wall. Nothing in her section of the bedroom gave any clue as to where she might have gone. The only thing that did strike him was how tidy the place looked: the bed was neatly made, no clothes lay over the back of the chair, and the top of her dresser seemed half empty. A photograph of her mother had gone.

He had a look in the sitting room and then Willa and Tom's bedroom. Standing on the mantelpiece was an envelope on which was written the one word 'Dad.' The handwriting was Stella's.

Calum took the envelope to the kitchen. He sat and looked at it and wondered what to do. He could not open it and did not know where Tom and Willa had gone. He would have to wait.

At midnight he heard them coming up the stairs. They were laughing. He met them at the door.

"I think Stella's run away." He held the letter out to Tom.

'Don't please try to find me,' she had written. 'I have gone to London. I have drawn all the money out of my post office book. I shall be all right.'

"London! Little idiot!" Tom was angry but also alarmed.

"You don't think she's really gone to London do you?" said Willa.

"Of course not! I bet she's gone out to Susie's."

"The key! Yes, I'm sure you're right, Tom."

Tom fished his car keys from his pocket.

"I'll come with you," said Willa. "You'll hold the fort, Calum?"

121

They ran down the stairs, their feet making a noise on the stone steps. The bottom door banged.

Betsy began to cry.

"Sore tummy."

"You ate too much."

"Want Mummy."

"She's not here."

"Want Stella."

"She's not here either."

He gave her a hot water bottle and she drifted back into sleep. He wandered about the flat going from room to room looking out of each window in turn. Lights in the other flats had dwindled, the sound of traffic was spasmodic rather than steady. He watched a drunk stagger up the pavement and collapse under a lamppost.

The telephone rang making his heart jump.

"Calum?" It was Tom. "She hasn't come back has she?"

"No."

"We're at Susie's." Tom sounded defeated. "She's not here."

Chapter Sixteen

Stella lay in her sleeping bag under the hedge at the back of the field watching the lights in the cottage. Tom and Willa had arrived in the car about an hour before. She had seen the headlights come along the road and then penetrate the drive and pick out the cottage.

They had slammed the car doors and run to open the cottage door calling out her name as they went. She had known they would be bound to come and check out the cottage: that was why she had taken refuge under the hedge. She would stay here until they left.

Tom appeared on the doorstep carrying a torch. She held her breath. He went into the garage and outhouses and the little toolshed, flashing the light in front of him. She did not think he would search the field. She was right.

A few minutes later the windows went black in the cottage. Tom and Willa came out together and stood for a minute in the middle of the garden. They seemed to be listening. Then they got into the car and drove off.

Stella waited until the sound of the car died away and for several minutes afterwards before she moved. She wriggled out of the bag and stood upright. An owl hooted, leaves rustled and whispered, some small animal scuttled through the undergrowth. The vast black sky was broken by a few stars. There was no moon. Something black flew low close to her right hand side. A bat perhaps. The night was full of sound and movement. She shivered. She felt alone in the middle of the earth.

Clutching the sleeping bag under one arm and her rucksack under the other, she made for shelter. The key turned easily in the lock. The door swung open and she was inside, ramming home the bolt and catching her breath. She could hear her heart thundering.

She knew the interior of the cottage well. She groped her way around, her eyes gradually becoming accustomed to the darkness until they could make out vague shapes. She dared not risk switching on the light in case someone passed in the road. Country folk seemed to notice everything. In the city you could send flares out of the window and most people would not notice.

Overhead was a loft reached by a pull-down ladder. She stood on a stool, felt for the end of the ladder, tugged and brought it carefully down between her hands. She climbed upwards into the dark.

By the time she had pulled the ladder back up and closed the trap door she was exhausted. It had been a very long evening. She spread out the sleeping bag and crawled in.

Sun streaming through the skylight on to her face wakened her. She jerked upright and glanced around, wondering where she was. Then she remembered and lay back. The ceiling sloped down close to her feet. The loft was used for storage; trunks stood by the back wall, boxes and pieces of furniture filled most of the remaining space. On many a wet afternoon she had raked through the trunks taking out old dresses and hats that had belonged to her grandmother. She would dress up and come down to show herself to Aunt Susie and Uncle Nick. She liked the musty smell of the clothes and the yellowed look of the old theatre programmes. Sometimes she had thought it would be nice to live up here.

She did not expect of course to live up here for ever. She was not so stupid as to think that she would be able to do that. But if she could survive for a while—even a week or two—by then Aunt Susie and Uncle Nick might be back from America. They might come back if her father was to telephone and tell them she was missing. And if they did then they would see how impossible it was for her to live any longer with the MacLeods and they would let her stay with them.

Her watch said ten minutes past nine. She must go downstairs now in case Tom and Willa returned.

Before touching anything below she watched from each window to make sure that no one was around. She ran water for as short a time as possible and after she had flushed the lavatory waited anxiously for the noise to die away. She could not run the risk of cooking in case the smell lingered or the hot plate retained enough warmth for someone to know that it had been used recently.

Aunt Susie's larder was full of tins and packets. Into a plastic bag Stella put a packet of cornflakes, tins of evaporated milk, orange juice and peaches, a packet of biscuits, a tin opener, cup, plate and spoon. Without hurrying or panicking she climbed back into the loft. She no longer felt excited. All her movements were calm and deliberate. She had done what she wanted to do and everything had gone smoothly.

When she had left home the evening before she had taken the bus from the station to a point on the main road some five miles away from the cottage. There had been no one on the bus she recognised. The top deck of the bus had been almost empty and she had sat at the front slumped well down in the seat.

During the five mile walk she had kept to the edge of the road and whenever she had heard a car approach had dived for cover. It was not a busy road but even so she had had to jump into the middle of woods or crouch behind a dry stone dyke sufficiently often for it to slow her progress and make the journey seem twice as long as usual.

She sat with her back against an old leather trunk which was plastered with stickers from countries all round the world, and ate her breakfast. She was starving, could have eaten the trunk itself, stickers and all. It seemed a long time ago since she had eaten chicken and chips in the kitchen with Calum and Betsy. A lifetime ago.

Now they could all move into the new flat and live happily ever after together.

It was getting the flat—something she had never really imagined Tom and Willa managing to do—that had finally made her decide to leave. She had realised then that there was no hope of them deciding they had made a mistake and that it would be better for everyone if they were to split up and each family go its separate way. They were determined to turn them into one big happy family.

After eating she fell asleep again and some hours later came to feeling heavy and hot. She took a drink of orange juice. It tasted warm. The air was thick and stuffy. Standing up she raised the skylight an inch or two and let the fresh air flow on to her face.

Then she lifted the trap door and peered down. Motes of dust danced in the sunlight. All was quiet. And safe. She lowered the ladder.

Once she had rinsed her face she felt better. She did a few limbering up exercises to ease the feeling of constriction in her arms and legs. From the bathroom she went then to the sitting room to do a reconnaissance.

For a moment she thought she would faint. Someone with dark red hair was coming along the road on a bicycle. It was Calum. She watched him come closer, unable, it seemed, to move.

She *must* move. Fast!

She ran back to the hall, took hold of the ladder and began to climb. The water cistern was still filling; the noise was enormous. Like a giant waterfall. The rope

126

swung to and fro. Steady, she told herself, don't panic. She clambered through the opening hauling the ladder up after her and placed the trap door in position. Calum would not know about the loft, nor would he be able to get into the house even if he had a key since she had bolted the door.

She lay on the floor with her ear close to the trap door. She thought she heard a key turn.

"Stella!" His voice reached her, muffled. He was banging on the front door.

Silence. Would he give up and go away?

He had gone round to the back door. he banged on that too and called her name again, and again.

"Go away and leave me alone, Calum MacLeod!" she whispered. He really *must* be mentally defective if he thought he could persuade her to go meekly home with him.

She listened to the sound of her own heart and the ticking of the watch on her wrist. He didn't appear to be doing anything now. Was he going away?

Then she heard the noise of breaking glass. It was like an explosion somewhere below her. She felt herself begin to shake. To steady herself she sank her teeth into the flesh of her forearm.

He was downstairs moving around, going from room to room. It would not take long to search the place: there were only four rooms and all were low and small. She almost thought she could hear him breathing.

His feet stopped.

She saw the trap door slowly rising. She pushed down on it hard.

"Stella, come down. *Please!*"

He was in the kitchen filling the electric kettle when she went.

"Why did you have to come here?" she cried. "Why couldn't you leave me alone?"

"Because I was worried about you. So is everybody.

The police are looking for you."

"You didn't have to come though, did you?"

"Yes I did. It's my fault, isn't it?"

"No. Not at all." The fire had gone out of her: she felt deflated, like a balloon that had lost its air.

He spooned coffee into two mugs, pierced a hole in a tin of milk.

"Come and have a cup of coffee."

She followed him into the sitting room.

"It won't do any good making me come back with you."

"*I* can't make you can I?"

"No, but I suppose the police could."

"Yes, I suppose they could. But do you really think Tom and Willa would send them out to collect you?"

They drank their coffee and looked out at the field.

Out there, in the corner of the garden, Hamish lay buried. Calum saw that grass was growing over the bald patch. He didn't intend to go and stand beside the grave and observe two minutes' silence or anything like that. He wanted to remember Hamish as he was in his head, not being lowered into a hole in the ground.

He looked back at Stella.

There were so many things he wanted to say to her but didn't know how to say them. He wanted to say that he knew how she felt and was sorry for he had felt all the same things in the past and still felt them sometimes. He wanted to say that he wanted her to be friends with Felicity again but that he couldn't give Felicity up for her sake. Felicity had been crying that morning. "Tell her to come home if you find her," she had said.

"Felicity—"

"I don't want to hear about Felicity," said Stella fiercely. She was like a wild cat when she was fierce. Always before when she had been like that he had drawn back.

"Yes, you do," he said.

128

"How do *you* know?"

"I just know, Stella."

How could *he* know what she wanted? They were as different as oil and water: that was what Aunt Ethel who had a saying for everything would say. She wished he would go away but he wouldn't, he was so stubborn he would just sit there until she gave in. Well, she wouldn't give in! Not for him anyway. If the police were to come along and drag her home then she supposed she'd have to go in the end. But she'd put up a fight for it. She'd kick and scream. She wouldn't listen to their pleas to come quietly. Come on now, lass, be reasonable. . .

She didn't feel reasonable, not one little bit.

"Why don't you go home?" she demanded. "It isn't your fault that your mother and my father got married."

"No. But that's not the only problem is it? There's Felicity—"

"And maybe it's not your fault either that Felicity Hall fell madly in love with you!"

He blushed. She watched the colour rise up to the roots of his dark red hair. She wondered if his temper was going to rise with it. He did not move.

It was quite still outside. Nothing stirred in the field or on the road. Calum let his eye travel right along it and back. He had asked Willa and Tom not to come. "Give me a chance. Let me try to find her. Let me try to talk to her."

Tom had spent the day pacing up and down calling himself a fool and a failure. He had said he was a fool not to have noticed that Stella was so disturbed. And he had failed her as a father.

Willa had said they had been selfish and self-centred and that they should have realised it would be more difficult for the children to adjust.

"We did realise though," Tom had said and stopped in his pacing, looking bewildered. "We did try, Willa.

129

People say kids are adjustable."

"Maybe not as much as we thought. Or hoped."

Why did Tom and Willa have to talk so much? They went over and over the same things until they ended up back at square one. But that was how they were. And they were both like that, whereas Dave MacLeod liked to take a decision and get on with it.

They are suited, Willa and Tom, thought Calum. They would probably always argue and swing up and down but it would not matter.

"You don't give up just because of a few arguments, Calum," Willa had said to him.

He didn't even have an argument going with Stella: they were not talking at all. They were each locked into their own thoughts. But their thoughts were running close together. Suddenly, Calum realised that because they were he didn't have to say all the things he had wanted to say. Which he had planned to say, as he had pedalled the fifteen miles out here on Richard Hall's bike.

"Look, Stella," he said, and felt very strong and sure of himself. "I *do* understand. More than anyone else. Can't you see that?"

She glanced up and their eyes met. For the first time since they had met six months before they looked straight at one another.

He saw her pale face and dark eyes which were so full of confusion and uncertainty.

She saw his amber-coloured eyes which were full of concern. For her. Yes, for her! They were steady eyes, like Felicity's grey ones.

Felicity. Stella thought about Felicity. Then she thought about her father. And about Willa.

"We're in this together, you know," said Calum.

He waited.

A fly buzzed against the window pane. The day was building up to be hot.

Stella nodded.

"Yes, we are, aren't we?" she said.

Calum gave her a little smile and leaned back in his chair.